D0009979

ALSO BY NIC STONE

For Middle-Grade Readers
Clean Getaway

For Teen Readers
Dear Martin
Odd One Out
Jackpot
Dear Justyce

NIC STONE

Crown Books for Young Readers
New York

Text copyright © 2021 by Logolepsy Media Inc.
Jacket art and interior illustrations copyright © 2021 by Noa Denmon

All rights reserved. Published in the United States by Crown Books for Young Readers, an imprint of Random House Children's Books, a division of Penguin Random House LLC, New York.

Crown and the colophon are registered trademarks of Penguin Random House LLC.

Visit us on the Web! rhcbooks.com

Educators and librarians, for a variety of teaching tools, visit us at RHTeachersLibrarians.com

Library of Congress Cataloging-in-Publication Data
Name: Stone, Nic, author.
Title: Fast pitch / Nic Stone.
Description: First edition. | New York: Crown Books for Young Readers, [2021] | Audience: Ages 8–12. | Audience: Grades 3–7. | Summary: "Shenice Lockwood dreams of leading the Fulton Firebirds to the U12 softball regional championship. But Shenice's focus gets shaken when her great-uncle Jack reveals that a career-ending and family-name-ruining crime may have been a setup. It's up to Shenice to discover the truth about her family's past—and fast—before secrets take the Firebirds out of the game forever"—Provided by publisher.
Identifiers: LCCN 2021015096 (print) | LCCN 2021015097 (ebook) | ISBN 978-1-9848-9301-7 (hardcover) | ISBN 978-1-9848-9302-4 (lib. bdg.) | ISBN 978-1-9848-9303-1 (ebook)
Subjects: CYAC: Softball—Fiction. | Families—Fiction. | Racism—Fiction. | African Americans—Fiction.
Classification: LCC PZ7.1.S7546 Fas 2021 (print) | LCC PZ7.1.S7546 (ebook) | DDC [Fic]—dc23

The text of this book is set in 11.75-point Berling Std.
Interior design by Andrea Lau

Printed in the United States of America
10 9 8 7 6 5 4 3 2 1
First Edition

For Glenda F. Alexander, my beloved Granny A.

Thank you for having zero problem with us watching
The Sandlot basically every day.

1

Batter Up

We *have to win this game. . . .*
Like *gotta* win. No other option.

I've been playing base-related ball—first tee, now soft—since the minute I could hold up a bat. Just like my daddy. And his daddy before him. And *his* daddy before him. It's in my blood. And I learned the meaning of "love/hate relationship" in a game situation like this one.

It's the bottom of the sixth and we're up by three, but the opposing team is at bat. Bases are loaded, two strikes, two outs. Any time I say something is *stress-ful*, my mama rolls her eyes and says, "You're twelve,

Shenice. You have no idea what that word means." But this? Is stressful.

As I drop back into my squat behind home plate, my eyes scan the field, and I inhale deep. Impossible to *not* notice—for me at least—how different our two teams look. While every player on mine, the Fulton Firebirds, has some shade of brown skin, *all* of the Stockwood Sharks girls are white.

Which is the case for *most* teams in the 12U division of the Dixie Youth Softball Association. *DYSA*, if you're feeling fancy.

Not only are we Fulton Firebirds the first all-Black team in this league—which even considering the name is a huge deal—we're the *only* team in the entire DYSA with more than three Black players on the roster.

Across eight states. All of which were on the pro-slavery side during the Civil War. Something my daddy reminds me of every time he sees "DYSA."

"It's a weight no one your age should have to carry, but can't ignore," he says. And he's right: Every win feels . . . *historical.*

I hate it . . . but also love it.

Victory is almost ours.

I hear the ump—a short dude whose middle is shaped like the highlighter-hued ball that gives this game I love so much its name—hock a loogie above my head. It slams into the dirt on my right with the force of a slimy bullet.

So gross.

I breathe in again, though it definitely makes me feel like the hot dog I ate earlier is going to join ump guy's blob of mucus beside me. The air *has* to be full of phlegm germs right now.

I gotta get my head back in the game. Yes, we're up, but I'd be lying if I said the Sharks aren't good.

They're *real* good, in fact.

But so are we.

We have to win this game.

Their best batter is at the plate—Steph Mahoney. I know her name because of her rep as a home-run hitter. Not surprising once you see the latest Louisville Slugger LXT choke-gripped between her half-covered hands. Her batting gloves are fingerless, which I've never seen in our league. But considering that bat costs 350 bucka-roos, it's clear good ol' Steph is serious about this sport.

I lock gazes with our pitcher, Cala "Quickfire" Kennedy. My "teammate" since the days of rolling one of Daddy's baseballs back and forth in our shared playpen (though we haven't always played on the same *actual* team). She's the best, most epic fast-pitch heat thrower in the state. Likely even in all of *Dixie*, and maybe the whole country.

All she's gotta do is throw one more strike.

In my peripheral vision, I see the blond, freckly-faced girl on third base take a quick peek at her coach, who tugs at his right earlobe, and then brushes a finger beneath his nose. After a slight nod, she subtly steps one foot off the slightly raised white square, and shifts into a ready-to-run stance, eyes on Cala, like a little lion cub who has decided home plate is her prey.

Steal a run? Not on my watch.

We HAVE to win this game.

I "adjust" my face mask with my left hand—my signal to Hennessey Lane, our go-to third-base girl (and a robotics champion to boot), that the ball is coming at her fast so she can pick the runner off, which would win us the game—and within a second, Quickfire has thrown a pitch. It's wide, and Steph rightly doesn't swing. But I was right about blondie: she takes off from third.

Good thing they don't call me Lightning Lockwood for nothing. Before the ump can shout, *"Ball two!"* I've fired the yellow sphere at Hennessey, and the golden-haired Shark is diving back toward the base, her fingertips reaching the edge a mere breath before Hennessey tags her side, ball in glove.

"SAFE!" the third-base ump says, slashing his arms out to his sides.

Hennessey lobs the ball back to Cala, and as the LXT batter repositions herself, I use my fingers to signal my

4

suggested pitch: rising curve, outside edge. Cala stands, centers, and whips her arm around quick as a camera flash. It hits my glove before I can blink—

"BALL THREE!" Loogie Ump barks behind me. His voice *is* a little phlegmy. It's like I can *feel* the germs raining down on my back now.

"All good, Cay!" Cala's mom shouts from the stands. "Head in the game, baby!"

As I remove the ball from my glove to toss it back to Cala, it feels like it's on fire. Not *literally*, of course. But I have no doubt Cala feels it, too: this pitch could decide the game. All she's gotta do is throw one more strike.

I signal for a fastball, straight up the middle.

Cala lets it rip, and I position my glove and await the telltale *thunk* and slight throb of my palm inside my glove.

There's a *THWACK* instead. Followed by a different *thunk*: that of the Louisville Slugger hitting the ground. Steph takes off running, her orangey-red braid swinging as cheering explodes from the visitor stands.

I shoot to my feet and yank my helmet off. Watch, unable to breathe, as our center fielder, Britt-Marie Hogan—my best girl friend—runs with everything she's got to keep up with the soaring yellow ball . . .

She jumps, but to no avail. It flies over the fence, and the Shark fans yell even louder.

"HOME RUN!" the ump shouts behind me.

I turn away from the plate. There's no way I can *watch* us lose.

The ride home is super uncomfortable, largely because no one is saying a word inside the Firebus. Usually we all love being in Coach Nat's giant van—the whole team rides together to and from games, and the Firebus has space for all of us: thirteen players, plus Coach Nat and her wife, Ms. Erica, who never misses anything we do as a team.

Coach is the dean of a charter school in the "inner city" (she always puts that in quotes) and is an *actual* former youth softball national champion. She started the Fulton Firebirds two years ago at the suggestion of her mentor, a Black businesswoman we call Ms. Monica, who is the head lawyer at Coke, and who also is a former softballer. As Ms. Monica told us the first time we met her, "There just isn't enough *concentrated* Black girl magic in this sport." Coach Nat recruited every one of us from all over the city. And she and Ms. Erica take excellent care of us and are *very* invested in our team.

Example: they strung LED lights around the ceiling of the van—red, orange, and yellow, our team colors— and there's a rotating softball Ms. Erica covered in square mirrors hanging at the center that makes the colored light scatter everywhere. The outside of the van is black, but it has a firebird painted on the hood, with wings that turn to flames as they wrap around the sides.

Definitely the coolest vehicle on any road in *this* area of town. Which is kind of funny, because even though Coach Nat and Ms. Erica would fit in around here—they're both white ladies—we've all seen more than a few *other* white people notice who's driving this "drip mobile," as Coach Nat calls it, and do a double take. Makes us laugh every time.

Nobody is laughing now, though.

On a *win* day, we'd be talking and laughing and begging Ms. Erica to crank up the music since Coach Nat won't (she says it'll ruin our hearing).

We'd be singing and dancing. Celebrating.

But as we zip up the tree-lined highway out of "Sandy Saltshaker"—it's really Sandy *Springs*, but according to Britt-Marie, "In a place with so few people of color, the name should reflect the folks who live there so everyone *knows*"—it's so quiet, I feel like I can hear the germs from Loogie Ump's spit crawling around on my skin.

We stop at a red light, and I close my eyes and let my chin drop. Mama would say I'm being dramatic, and my numbskull little brother would toss in his unwanted two cents and agree, but I feel like my head has gotten too heavy for my neck and I just can't hold it up anymore.

I shouldn't cry. I know I shouldn't. Really, this isn't *that* big a deal. This game was basically a scrimmage. It won't hurt our record in the league or affect our standings as we head into tournament season a few weeks from now. It won't keep us from my *ultimate* goal for the team this year: the DYSA 12U World Championship title (even though "world" is clearly inaccurate since the whole league is only eight states). A team with a Black player—let alone an all-Black team—has never made it through the district tournament. Even making it to State would be huge: a message that girls like us *do* belong on the field. We've definitely had some games where the opposing team's fans suggested otherwise. Gotta love Georgia.

Going all the way—snagging that *Dixie* trophy—would be next level.

But to get there, we have to actually *win*.

I feel like such a baby about the jawbreaker lump in my throat that feels like it's gonna dissolve and spill outta my eyes in liquid form. Especially since I know getting eaten by the Stockwood Sharks doesn't. Actually. MATTER.

Still, though: The other girls in the creepily silent van voted to make *me* their captain. It's my job to keep morale up . . . and I can't think of a single thing to say.

Because it's also my job to lead us to victory, and I clearly failed at that, too.

The jawbreaker liquid is spilling over now. Too bad it's not sweet instead of salty.

An arm slips beneath *my* left arm—the one I catch with—and hooks my elbow before something heavy lands on my shoulder.

Britt-Marie's head.

"I'm pretty sure my eyesight is ruined from the sun glistening off all that shiny golden hair," she says.

I snort.

"I'm serious," she continues. "They had a *blinding* advantage. The kajillion-dollar super bats didn't hurt, either."

"You're ridiculous, Britt," I say, smiling now.

"I'm right. And you know it."

I don't say anything back. Don't have to. I just breathe out and let the trees blur by.

2

Home Team

Sunday mornings in the Lockwood household are usually my favorite time of the week. We're not churchgoers unless it's Easter, Juneteenth, or Christmas, and there typically aren't any weekly plans or activities, so my brother Drake and I sleep until eleven and wake to the smell of bacon.

And to old-people music. There's this one group called Boyz II Men that sings a lot of sappy songs our parents seem to love dancing and being ooey-gooey to. They hug all up on each other, and they kiss. On the mouth. And while there's technically nothing *wrong* with kissing—I haven't done it yet, but a couple girls on the team have, and they seem to like it—seeing my parents do it is . . . yuck.

Especially this morning.

"Could you guys maybe get a room?" I say as I step into the kitchen. Mama is sitting on the island, and Daddy's in front of her with one arm around her waist. They're just smoochin' away like nobody else lives here.

Daddy pulls back. "Last I checked, *we* have an entire house," he says. "You certainly don't pay any bills up in here."

"Mm-hmm," Mama chimes in. I can imagine her dark brown eyes cutting to the side, and her full lips pursing. "Freeloaders stay *full* of opinions, don't they, baby?" She pulls his face back toward hers.

"They sure do, queen."

And then they're at it again.

"So nasty," I grumble, plopping down at the kitchen table.

"Who pooed in your Cheerios?" My head flies forward—a result of being pushed from behind—and I swing my throwing arm. My annoying little brother, Drake, manages to jump out of the way, completely dodging the blow.

"*STEEE-RIKE!*" He laughs and takes the seat across the table from me.

"You're childish," I say. "Sneak attacks are cowardly. And who even says *pooed*?"

"I do! POOOOOOED!"

"Child. Ish."

"I mean, I *am* a child. . . ."

"You're *both* children, and we can tell," Mama says. She sets plates of steaming scrambled cheese eggs, French toast, golden hash brown rounds, and fried green tomatoes on the table. Then she goes back to the kitchen and returns with a bowl I know is full of piping-hot pimento cheese grits, and a platter of thick Black Forest bacon.

I smile, knowing *this* bacon—the only bacon Millie Lockwood allows to touch her precious seasoned cast-iron griddle—involves a forty-seven-minute drive outside the city to a farmer's market in what Britt-Marie would call "questionable territory." And she's not entirely wrong: I've made the trip with Mama a few times, and we do see a number of Confederate flag emblems on billboards, in yards, and on the bumpers of cars along the way.

But the farmer we buy our bacon from? Mr. Joiner? He's one of the nicest old white dudes I've ever met. In fact, last time I went with Mama, he showed me a *signed* Satchel Paige baseball card—*super* old-school, and so original, he had it in a thick plastic sleeve. And he told me that if I lead my team to the State title, he'll give it to me. To keep.

Mama puts our beverages of choice in front of our place settings: sparkling water for her; coffee for

Daddy . . . as in the whole pot; orange juice for Drake (so basic, that kid); and freshly squeezed star ruby grapefruit juice for me. Then she passes empty plates around and sits as Daddy slowly makes his way over. For as long as I can remember, he's walked with a cane, but it does seem like he's moving slower and is in more pain than usual these days. He groans as he takes his seat.

"Daddy, you okay?" I ask, temporarily distracted from my sour mood.

"Right as rain, Honeybee, right as rain." He rubs his hands together. "Looking forward to that bacon."

"Me too." Drake licks his lips. "Can we eat now?"

"How's your knee?" I continue to Daddy. "Hurting any more than usual?"

He looks at me and grins. "Depends on who wants to know."

"Hold that thought," Mama says. "Let's say grace and get to eating before Li'l Man inhales the table."

"Ma, you *gotta* stop calling me that."

"Boy, bye," she replies. "Now y'all bow your heads if you want this food."

I would never tell anyone, but my mind sometimes wanders when Mama is giving thanks for our food/life/health/family, etc. The smell of the bacon makes me think of Mr. Joiner, which makes me think of that Satchel Paige card, which makes me think of why Satchel Paige was famous in the first place: he was the first Black player to pitch in—and win—an MLB World Series. *This* makes me think of our team's championship goals. What's at stake and how big a deal it would be to win . . . which just reminds me of our loss to the Stockwood Sharks.

"Yes, Lord," Daddy replies to something Mama just said. And the sound of *his* voice gets my brain spinning in a different direction: Daddy blew his knee out stealing home during a tournament game when he played baseball in college. Not only did it end his season, it eliminated any chance he had of going pro. And the injury is *still* causing him problems.

Which would be bad enough if not for the fact that Daddy was trying to live out the dream *his* daddy—my PopPop—never got to achieve: no one was really paying Black players in the 1970s if they weren't in the Major Leagues, so when my granny got pregnant, PopPop had to "quit tossing balls around and get a real job." (He was still bummed out about it when he died a few years ago.)

And *PopPop* was apparently trying to live the dream for *his* daddy: my Great-Grampy Jon-Jon. Our family's baseball patriarch—

"Shenice?" Daddy's voice cuts into my thoughts. When I open my eyes, everyone is staring at me.

"Well?" Mama says.

Which is when I know the prayer is over. And they're

all waiting for me to say "Amen." This maybe happens more often than I want to admit, though this morning, I'm kinda glad my thought train got stopped when it did.

"My bad," I say. "Amen."

Mama nods, and Drake launches himself forward and grabs the plate of bacon like he hasn't had food in a hundred years.

Our brunch rolls on without a hitch and with (mostly) typical Lockwood Sunday chitchat—a few gratitude circles, where we pass a plate around and say things we're thankful for; talk about our goals for the week ahead; updates on the lives of distant family members Drake and I have never met (Mama and Daddy); fart jokes between Drake and me, and the fussing from Mama that always comes after (while Daddy secretly laughs behind his napkin).

There's no mention of my softball loss, and I'm honestly too relieved to think anything of it. But then I look up and catch Daddy giving me what I call the *Great Gaze*. It's this thing where he eyes a person with his left brow-bush slightly raised, and he stares right into the person's thoughts through the black parts of their eyeballs.

Or at least that's what it feels like to me.

And for good reason: of everybody in the universe, Daddy's the person who knows me best. Who can read me like a Virginia Hamilton book. Who sometimes knows what I'm feeling even before I do, and then helps me figure it out. I couldn't hide anything from him if I tried.

He's nice enough not to call me out at the table. I'm not in the mood for one of Mama's *You're the best at everything, always, even when you lose* pep talks. Nor do I want Drake cracking hidden reminder jokes ("This kid in my class totally *swung* and *missed* with this girl he likes," the little dork would say).

But the moment his napkin goes from his lap to the table, I know there's no avoiding what he refers to as a "Dad call-*in*."

"Drake, you're on dish duty this morning," he says.

Drake opens his mouth to protest: according to the meticulously kept calendar on the fridge, it's *my* week to clear the table and load the dishwasher. But little bro thinks better of it. Just sighs and mumbles, "Okay, Daddy."

Then, after a nod between Daddy and Mama that suggests some kind of telepathic connection (is that what happens when you've been married for like a century?), Daddy rises from the table.

And zeroes in on me.

"Lightning Lockwood, you come with me," he says. The sound of my nickname feels like seventy-two jillion vampire bats screeching right into my ear. The name was given to me by my teammates two years ago after I stole three bases and threw four outs in a single game, but I don't feel deserving of it after losing to the dumb Stockwood Sharks.

I get up and follow him out of the kitchen.

Neither of us says a word until I see him approaching the stairs that lead to the second floor, aka a place he never really goes because climbing is so painful for him. His and Mama's bedroom is on the ground level of our two-story, orange sherbet–colored house.

But then he props his cane on the floor and uses it and the railing for leverage as he begins the journey up. "Dad, you sure about those steps with that knee?" I ask, more to stall than anything.

"As I mentioned not too long ago, this is *my* house. Ain't no bum knee can stop me from going wherever I wanna go inside it."

He hasn't mentioned the game yet. Makes me nervous. "Yeah, but didn't the doctor who jabbed you in the leg with that giant needle tell you not to climb stairs? Even you said you want to avoid another one of those cortisone shots 'for a good long while.' "

"You gonna tattle on me, Neecie-Pop?" he groans as he takes the next step.

It makes my stomach flip.

"Dad, come on. We can talk downstairs. I don't mind Drake or Mama heari—"

"This is important, Shenice." Another step, another groan. "Need you to trust me."

"But where are we *going*?" I ask, definitely a little whinier than I'm proud of, but hey.

"Ah, you'll see," he says. "Just might take us a little longer to get there than you're used to."

3

Catch

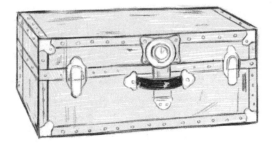

Once we reach the top of the stairs, and Daddy leans against the railing with his eyes closed to catch his breath, I have to ask: "Dad, when's the last time you were up here?"

"Friday morning," he says. "Now mind ya business and come on." He shifts his weight onto his cane and heads right.

Part of me is relieved: there are four rooms on this floor, and mine is at the opposite end of the hallway, across from Mama's office. Not that I have anything to *hide* were Daddy to be leading us to my room. It's just not as . . . "organized" as he'd say it should be. *"Especially for the captain of a softball team in pursuit of a league championship title, Miss Ma'am."*

(I hate when he calls me that. Almost as much as I hate the fact that we lost to those dang Stockwood Sharks.)

But then it hits me: if we're not headed to *my* side of the stairs . . .

"Are we going to Drake's room?" I say with a smile.

About my "little" brother: in truth, Drake is only fourteen months younger than me and just a year behind in school. But I emphasize the *little* because since I was in fifth grade and he was in fourth, he's been taller than me.

It's annoying.

He has epilepsy, but trust me when I say it doesn't keep him from being your typical annoying sixth-grade sibling.

Which is why the idea of going to *his* room is making me grin. I have zero doubt Drake's space would make mine look like I'd gotten a visit from the organizer lady on this TV show about "the bliss of living tidy." With the noise and chaos Drake brings into my life, there's no way his room—which I'm never allowed into—is in any kind of order.

"I'd be careful, if I were you," I say as we near the closed door. ("Your parents let you close doors?" three of my teammates said the first time they came over. "Mine would take the hinges off if I ever tried that." Definitely gave new meaning to one of Mama's favorite sayings: *Don't forget privacy is a privilege.*) "No telling what's in there."

He snorts . . . but then continues *past* the entrance to Drake's room on the left.

Which can only mean we're headed for the *always* closed door at the end of the hall on the right.

I gulp.

Pure honesty: I don't have a single, solitary clue what's behind that door. I *do* know that room once belonged to Daddy's dad, PopPop. He passed away when I was six, but I would be lying if I said I had many memories of him besides the one where he told me why he stopped playing baseball. Even when Drake and I were little, and PopPop was alive, we weren't really allowed in his room. PopPop was very sick and died from colon cancer.

The space has been off-limits for as long as I can remember. And I've never dared to even crack the door and peek inside. I'm almost 100 percent sure Drake hasn't, either. Which is saying a lot for him. In fact, half the time, I forget there *is* a room over here that's not Drake's.

When Daddy steps in front of it and reaches for the old-school crystal doorknob—this is the only room my parents didn't gut and renovate when they decided to make "home upgrades" when I was in third grade— I stop a good six feet back.

My fingertips tingle. I feel silly about it, but what if it's like . . . a portal to another dimension or something? Or maybe Daddy will open the door and snow will come out. Are we about to cross into Narnia? (Not that I still *believe* in all that fairy-tale stuff . . .)

"Wait!" I say as he reaches for the knob. Has it always been that *sparkly*?

Daddy looks at me, and I have no clue what expression he sees on my face, but both of his bushy brows shoot up. "You good?"

"I'm not allowed in there," I say, unable to pull my eyes from his hand. Am I *scared*? I'm totally scared. So glad none of my teammates can see me right now. Some mighty leader *I* am . . .

There's gonna be snow. I just know it. "That room is off-limits," I remind him.

At this, Daddy smiles. "Well, you have my permission today, Miss Ma'am."

(Ugh.)

"I meeeean . . . I'm *good*, Dad. Like, *really*. Don't need permission because I wouldn't wanna defile such a sacred space. You know? We can head back downstairs. Sorry you made the climb for nothin—"

"Girl, if you don't get your tail over here." He turns the knob, and my breath totally gets stuck in my throat. "I told you this is important. Now come on."

He shoves the door open. . . .

No snow.

Well, none coming *out* of the room, at least. Daddy steps in, and I slowly get closer.

"Need ya to pick up the pace a little bit, Lightning Lockwood," he says from inside. "You asked about my knee earlier, and I didn't say a whole lot, but after all of those stairs, my *sit-down* timer is ticking. And we got one more set to get up."

At that, I force myself through the doorway and glance around the space: it's . . . a bedroom. That looks like it belonged to a grandparent. There's tan paisley wallpaper and a queen-sized four-poster bed with a knitted afghan folded and draped across the bottom. Antique-looking dark wood dresser with a big mirror against the wall directly opposite the bed, and a small desk with a lamp and a cup of pens. (When's the last time anybody used one of those?)

The most surprising thing isn't the normalness of the room, though.

It's the fact that in the wall to my left, there's another door. Daddy is standing beside it, holding it open. There are stairs beyond it.

"Go on up," Daddy says.

So I do. And though what I find at the top isn't exactly Narnia, it's definitely close enough for me.

It takes Daddy some time to get up the staircase, so I'm able to stand and take in the space by myself for a bit. It's dustier than the room below, and there are some cobwebs, but it's plain as day that this was once some kind of "man cave," as Daddy would put it. (*"So* sexist," I can hear Britt-Marie saying in my head.)

There is baseball paraphernalia all over the place: framed posters—all signed—tacked up on the slanted walls, a case full of plaques and trophies, and a rack of variously sized old-school Louisville Slugger bats. There are also framed newspaper pages and what looks like the sort of diploma certificate I got at fifth-grade graduation.

In the center of the room, there's a leather reclining chair. And then I spot . . . "Whoa."

"You're right about that," Daddy says, waving the air in front of his face. "Might have to change my policy and allow Miss Caroline up here so she can dust." (Miss Caroline is the woman who does a "deep clean" of our house once per month. Drake and I are still responsible for our own rooms, though.)

But my *whoa* has nothing to do with the dust. Because

in the far corner, there's a big trunk. One I would've *sworn* didn't actually exist.

Daddy starts making his way toward it.

"Is that . . . ?"

"That's it." He stops in front of it and smiles. "Your Great-Grampy JonJon's infamous trunk."

"You mean it's *real?*"

At this, Daddy laughs. But I'm being serious.

Despite not really spending any time with PopPop, I do remember crying when Mama and Daddy came to tell Drake and me that he'd passed.

I cried so hard, in fact, Daddy gave me something he said I wasn't supposed to get until after the funeral: a big clover-topped key made of the same stuff as Mama's favorite skillet—cast iron.

"This key opens your Great-Grampy JonJon's special trunk," he said. "Your PopPop kept it safe for a loooooong time, and he asked me to pass it to you to do the same. That way *both* men live on inside you. You're carrying their legacies."

It's why I got so serious about softball.

At first, I would constantly ask when I could see the trunk and use the key. Daddy would always respond, "When it's time, it'll be time, kiddo."

After hearing that for maybe the *fiftieth* time, and learning more about my family's baseball legacy, it occurred to me that the trunk might not be real. And I was strangely okay with that. By then I'd accepted that "bat-ball," as Drake puts it, was in my seven-year-old blood, so there not being a real trunk didn't negatively impact my game.

Then when we started learning about symbolism in Mr. Bonner's language arts class this year—*a concrete representation of a thing or idea that is more abstract in nature*—it clicked: the trunk *wasn't* an actual trunk. It was a symbol of my grandfather's and great-grandfather's legacies. And I held the literal key.

Well, almost literal . . . there doesn't seem to be an actual lock. So perhaps it is also symbolic. (Mr. Bonner would be so proud of this "literary analysis.")

But now my daddy is standing over a *literal* trunk.

Staring at me.

Grinning.

Then he opens the lid . . . and within moments, I'm looking down into what definitely qualifies as a treasure. Feels like my heart has stopped beating.

There are well-worn wooden bats similar to the ones on the rack (Great-Grampy JonJon clearly had a *lot* of bats), baseballs ranging from brand-new to gently beige to scuffed and grimy with unraveling red seams, four pairs of old cleats, and a few trophies and stacks of plaques with the name JonJon Lee Lockwood etched into their faces. There are two pairs of old batters' gloves and a slightly dried-out glove for fielding—the type of glove people think about when they hear the word "baseball"— and there's a deliciously worn catcher's mitt.

Like I said: a treasure.

Two things stand out: 1. A framed black-and-white photo of who I assume is Great-Grampy JonJon (in uniform) standing with a man I don't recognize, and 2. What looks like a fancy leather journal. Like one with the attached strings that wrap around and tie it shut.

Daddy clears his throat beside me. But I can't seem to pull my eyes away from that notebook.

Until there's something literally blocking my view.

It takes me a second to figure out what Daddy is trying to give me, but once I do . . .

"Wait," I say. "I thought Great-Grampy JonJon was a left fielder."

"Most of the time, yes. But he also did some catching." Daddy pushes the catcher's mitt toward me, and I swear my hands heat up as they make contact with the thing.

Daddy goes on: "That loss yesterday burned you up. I could tell the moment you stepped outta the team van."

Tears pop into the corners of my eyes instantly.

"And it's hard. Lord knows *I* know how hard it is. It was hard for me as the only spot of color on the diamond throughout my baseballing years, hard for your

PopPop, and *very* hard for your Great-Grampy JonJon. You shouldn't *have* to feel the things you do on that field. But there's no helping it."

"Yeah," I manage.

"You got big dreams. And if *anyone* can lead your team to a championship title, it's you, Lightning Lockwood. It's in your blood. That's why I brought you up here. So you could *see* that," Daddy goes on. "Just gotta dust yourself off and get your head back in the game."

I sigh. I'm holding Great-Grampy JonJon's buttery-soft mitt (this thing is *perfectly* broken in) that was pulled from a trunk I didn't think was real, and handed to me by a man who is struggling to stand after climbing *two* flights of stairs. One of which I didn't know *existed*, even though I've lived in this house my whole life.

Is any of this really happening?

"When you were little and you would ask about this trunk, I would tell you . . . do you remember?"

"When it's time, it'll be time," I say.

He nods. "I know you can't *use* this because it's far too big. But think of it as a reminder of what's *in* you, baby girl."

My eyes drop back to the photo of JonJon and the other man. Then shift to the leather journal.

"The time is now, Shenice." He puts a hand on my shoulder, and I look up at him. "Let 'em see whatcha got."

And he winks.

4

Strike One

As honored as I am to have received Great-Grampy JonJon's mitt, all I've been able to think about since Daddy closed the trunk is that little brown book I saw inside of it.

I spend most of dinner wondering what it could be. It *looked* like a journal. Or maybe it's a ledger: though he's gone digital now, Daddy used to keep a physical ledger for the pair of hardware stores he owns, and the little number-filled volumes were similar in size and shape to the book in the trunk.

Or maybe it's full of to-do lists. Or baseball statistics.

The most pressing question of all: Did it *really* belong

to Great-Grampy JonJon? I go to bed clutching his catcher's mitt to my chest and thinking over what I actually know about him:

1. He fought in a war (not sure which one), and when he came back, he got serious about playing baseball.
2. He was really good and played in the Negro American League . . . or maybe it was the Negro Southern League?
3. According to Daddy, he was *almost* one of the first Black players recruited to the MLB. But something happened.

Nobody's ever told me what. And I never thought to ask because . . . I dunno. I guess it didn't seem to matter.

But now? The book creeps into my dreams and chases me around and around a softball diamond inside a field of lava. All night, I "do the flippity-floppity," as Mama used to say when I'd crawl into her and Daddy's bed as a little kid and squirm in my sleep.

What would it tell me about the man who started our family's "batball" legacy?

It's on my mind the next morning when I sit down to write in *my* journal, as I do every Monday through Friday before heading down to breakfast. The current one was a birthday gift from my (boy) best friend Scoob and is a favorite. The cover has flippable sequins: push them all up and it says TIME TO STRIKE, but if you flip them down, a lightning bolt appears.

I have excellent friends.

Anyway, I write about the book, thinking it'll clear my mind (isn't that what journaling is for?), but it doesn't work like it usually does. I wind up walking into the banister, and then almost fall down the stairs because I'm craning my neck to see PopPop's closed bedroom door.

Daddy grins at me throughout breakfast—which we have as a family as often as possible—and I'm able to focus on the conversation solely because it centers on my game tonight: our last district matchup. Which actually *matters* in our pursuit of that league championship title because it'll determine whether or not we make it into the section tournament.

But as I tie my shoes for school, my mind gets pulled away again: my brown shoelaces remind me of those leather strings wrapping the little brown book tight.

It's all down distraction hill from there.

When I first get to school, I not only walk right past Britt-Marie without speaking (which she is *not* cool with), I also blow right by Scoob. He has to chase me down and catch my arm before I turn a corner.

School itself is a wash. Even in my favorite class,

where I'm *always* tuned in—language arts with Mr. Bonner, a very tall, brown-skinned man who coaches the girls basketball team Laury and Cala play on in the winter—I struggle to focus. It's partially his fault, though. We're reading this book called *Monster,* and today's lesson is on symbolism: cue my realization that the key Daddy gave me was symbolic.

It makes me wonder what else I don't know about my family. About my great-grandfather. Didn't have the courage to ask Daddy why he stopped playing baseball this morning. I guess since finding out the trunk is real, and seeing inside of it, I'm a little nervous about all the things I don't know. I get like this sometimes when I think about how big the universe could be. All the *possibilities.*

It's why I'm stuck on that dang book.

What if it contains family secrets that make me question everything I know? Or something that makes me feel like my whole batball life has been a big lie? If the end of Great-Grampy JonJon's career was as simple as an injury like Daddy's, or not being able to support a family like PopPop's, someone would've told me.

Right?

What could be so bad a grown-up wouldn't tell a kid about it?

After school, I decide I'll squeeze some homework into my hour of free time before I need to get ready for the game, but when I pull a worksheet out of my folder, I realize I have no idea how to do the assignment because . . . well, I hadn't exactly been "fully engaged in the lesson," as Mr. Bonner would say.

I huff and slouch down in my desk chair. Kick off the floor and give myself a spin (rotating chairs for the win). I know full well that the thing I can't stop thinking about is literally down the hall, through two doors, and up a flight of stairs. I could have it in the palm of my hand in less than a minute.

But I can't bring myself to go into PopPop's room without permission. And I *also* know that if I ask for permission, there will be questions like *Why do you want to go in there?* and I definitely couldn't bring myself to lie about that. "*Integrity* is one of the most important qualities in a leader," Daddy's voice rings in my head. It's one of the first things he said to me when he found out I made captain.

And I feel kinda dumb about it—it's just an old *book*—but I also can't seem to let it go. So my wheels keep turning.

Through the change into my uniform: *Maybe it's a chronicle of some secret life Great-Grampy JonJon was living . . .*

Through the twenty-minute drive to meet the team: *Or maybe it's some kind of playbook that could change the face of all batball.*

And through the Firebus ride to the game, as the mirrored softball spins, so does my brain: *Maybe he was working on the cure for some disease. Or creating a schematic for an invention that would've shifted the world.*

Luckily, drives *to* games are usually pretty quiet, so no one notices that I'm totally checked out. But once we pile out of the van and head to the away-team dugout? When Coach Nat says, "Hey, Little Lightning, let me holler at you for a sec," I flinch so hard, my mitt goes flying and wallops Khyler Jenkins—Hennessey's robotics partner and our division's best shortstop by far—upside the head.

"Oh my god, I'm so sorry!"

"Oh your *goodness,*" Ms. Erica says over her shoulder as she pulls out the square Firebird cushions she makes us sit on. ("Can't have sore tushies distracting my winners!") She begins laying them out on the metal bench.

Everyone else, though, is just staring at me.

I clear my throat. "Got too much game on the brain!" And I force a laugh.

No one laughs back. Likely because Khyler is still rubbing the side of her head.

I stand up straighter. "Dust it off, Jenkins," I say, smacking Khyler on the back a little harder than I intend to. (Whoops!) "No harm, no foul. We got a game to win, don't we? Head in the flames!"

This is what we say instead of *Head in the game,*

since we're the Firebirds. A little corny, but it does the trick.

Without waiting for a response, I set my stuff down and follow Coach Nat out to the Firebus. "Quite a pep talk you gave back there, Captain," she says as she opens the rear doors and heaves out the team cooler. Hennessey's mom was in charge of snacks and drinks today, and she also works for Coke (in a different department than Ms. Monica), so I'm sure it's full of Powerade bottles and Dasani waters. "You doing all right?"

"I'm solid, Coach," I say, putting my game voice on. "Ready for this win."

She stretches out the fancy insulated bags packed with stuff like organic cheese cubes, carrot and celery sticks, and homemade hummus. But when I grab them, she doesn't let go.

"What's on your mind, kiddo?" she says, locking me in one of those coach stares that feel like she can see all my secrets. "You're a bit zoned out today." I drop my gaze from her blue eyes, which remind me of swimming pool water on a sunny day . . . and kind of creep me out a little.

Still can't lie to her. Not completely, at least. "Just some family stuff, Coach. Nothing to worry about."

One of her brown eyebrows ticks up, but she nods. "All right. I'll take you at your word, but don't forget we're here for you. Cool?"

"Yes, ma'am."

"Head in the flames?"

"Head in the flames," I repeat.

But my head is certainly *not* in the flames.

In fact, there's one point where I get so caught up looking at the other (completely white) team and thinking about what Great-Grampy JonJon might've had to deal with if he *had* gone to the MLB, Cala throws a perfect strike straight up the center of home plate, and I totally dodge instead of catching it. Which means the ump also has to dodge to keep from getting hit in the . . . Yeah, it would *not* have been pretty.

Thankfully, the Buford Barracudas are . . . not very barracuda-ish. Even with my head in the clouds instead of the flames—and certainly not in any sort of captain-mode—we Firebirds torch them. Final score: eight to three.

It's no thanks to me, but we're officially on our way to the section tournament. The post-game stop at Mellow Mushroom, where we celebrate all of our wins with pizza, and the Firebus ride back home are bananas—and I'm thankful: everyone's so happy we won, nobody asks me what was up.

But when I close my eyes to sleep that night, all I can see is that little brown book.

5

Changeup

On my mind when I wake up the following morning: how terrible I played in such a huge game.

"Why do you look like somebody corked your bat?" Drake says when he sits down across the breakfast table from me. "Didn't you guys win?"

"You clearly have no idea what a corked bat is, kid," I say.

But then halfway through the meal, Daddy picks up his coffee mug and taps his fork against it. Definitely doesn't *ping* the way I think he expects it to, but it does get our attention.

Even more attention-grabbing: him suddenly bursting into tears.

"Uhhh . . . ," I begin. But Mama shushes me.

"There, there, baby," she says, patting Daddy's massive hand. Takes everything in me to hold in the fit of nervous laughter I can feel bubbling up. The last time I saw Daddy cry was when PopPop died.

"I'm all right, I'm all right," he says. "I'm just . . ." He bites his lower lip. "I'm just so proud of my baby girl."

Oh, boy.

"Come over here, Lightning," he continues.

I gulp and comply. "Yes, Daddy?" I say once I'm standing in front of him.

He turns to me and slides the ring off of his right pinkie. "I want you to have this," he says.

And now I'm speechless. That's his high school baseball state championship ring.

"I was the first Black player on a state champion team. You just led the first all-Black team to a 12U softball district title. You earned this."

"Whoa" is all I can muster. And partially because I feel like it's a lie. I didn't really *lead* anybody to anything. If we're honest, my team sorta had to drag me along.

"You're bringing such honor to the Lockwood name, Shenice." More tears fall as Daddy closes my hand around the ring. "I know PopPop and JonJon are cheering their hearts out as they watch on from heaven."

"A-MEN," Mama says. She's crying, too.

The whole thing makes my stomach knot up.

It does get me back on track, though. I give it my all at practice on Tuesday. Which is saying a lot because it's a doozy—multiple cycles of around-the-horn drills followed by full-speed base laps, capped off with Coach Nat's favorite form of torture: push-ups. I even hit a gorgeous fly ball that arcs over our right fielder Noelle's head and *almost* reaches the fence.

"Great to have you back, Lightning," Coach says as I'm packing up.

Good feeling doesn't last long, though: when I step off the field, there's no sign of the powder-blue Cadillac convertible Daddy removes the cloth cover from and pulls out of the garage every spring. He calls it his baby girl (guess I'm chopped liver), though the car belonged to PopPop and is literally a year older than Daddy is.

The thing is impossible to miss. Which is how I know it's . . . missing.

"That's weird," I say, looking around.

Britt-Marie steps up beside me. "What, the janky dreadlocks on this park's white groundskeeper?"

"Oh my god, Britt—"

"*Goodness*," Ms. Erica says in passing. She's carrying a basket of neon-yellow softballs to the Firebus.

"I'm not wrong." She spots the guy on a riding lawn mower one field over. "It is absolutely *weird*."

I smack my forehead, and she shrugs.

"You know you agree with me, girl," she says. "Where's Papa Lockwood?"

"*That's* what I'm saying is weird," I reply. "He doesn't seem to be here."

"Huh. He's never late, though."

"I'm aware, Britt. It's why I said it's weird."

"*Weird* is such a weird word, isn't it?" She looks at her fingernails. Britt-Marie's nails are always perfectly polished. Today it's holographic silver glitter. She's definitely the most traditionally "girly girl" on our team. (Though anybody who said that aloud would get punched in the *least* traditionally "girly" way.) "Words in general are pretty weird. That someone just *decided* putting little symbols together in clumps was a way to make stuff have meaning? Super weird."

I turn to her. "It's like you're speaking . . . but I have no idea what you're *saying*."

"Oh, shut up," she replies.

Just then, a sleek red Volvo comes whipping into the parking lot, old-school music—something about not wanting "no scrub," whatever that means—pouring out the windows and filling the air like the thick exhaust from a dump truck.

"Mama?" I say aloud, though she certainly can't hear me.

Before she comes to a complete stop in front of us,

Britt-Marie is bounding toward the car. "Hi, Ms. Millie!" she says, leaning into the open passenger window. Something *weirder* than my daddy not being here: my best friend is obsessed with my mama. They talk hair products (all three of us have big, curly manes, though I'm definitely not as *into* mine as they are), "skin-care regimens," and baking recipes . . . all things I couldn't give a flip about. "Ooh, I *love* that twist-out!" Britt-Marie is saying. "Did you use that styling custard I suggested?"

"You know I did, baby girl!"

Now Mama is fluffing her hair. I swear Britt-Marie should just move in and replace me.

I pop the trunk and throw my stuff inside, then bump Britt-Marie out of the way so I can, you know, actually get in the car.

"Excuse you! Uncalled for," she says once I pull the door open. But then there's a honk behind us, and a bright blue four-door Jeep—though none of the doors are actually on the thing—propped up on massive tires screeches to a stop a *tad* too close to Mama's bumper.

Britt-Marie's stepbrother, Sebastian. Who Britt-Marie can't stand.

"Ugh, can I just go home with you guys?" she says, rolling her eyes so hard, it's a wonder they don't get stuck.

Which Mama apparently finds hilarious. "Girl, you are something else," she says to Britt-Marie. When I rolled *my* eyes over something last week, she reacted like I'd taken my bat to her great-grandmother's bone china, but whatever. "Normally I'd say yes," Mama goes on, "but we're not headed home just yet. We'll catch ya later!" And she throws up a peace sign.

"Mama, I love you," I say as we pull out of the parking lot, "but that peace sign thing you just did makes you look your age."

"Oh, you hush, Miss Ma'am."

Which reminds me . . . "Where's Daddy?"

"He's at the house."

I'm about to ask if something is wrong, but when we get to the stop sign, Mama takes a right instead of the left that would lead us home.

Hmm . . . "So, where are we going?" I say, more nervous than I'd care to admit. Daddy not picking me up from a Tuesday practice is like the sun not rising.

"You'll see," she says, pulling the ultimate mom card and patting my knee. "There's someone your daddy and I want you to meet."

It doesn't take long to reach our destination, but my heart is beating like I just ran a field lap for the whole ride. My parents aren't real big on *surprises*, so this is clearly a big deal. Should I maybe not be sweat-soaked and covered in dirt?

And I really am very sweaty. I can feel a drop rolling down my side as Mama takes a visitor parking space in front of a four-story brick building. Once we're out, I follow her across the lot to a long walkway, and I see the words **Peachtree Hills Place** carved in an arch over semi-fancy double doors.

As we approach them, Mama speaks. "I know your daddy gave you your great-grandad's catching mitt," she says. "And I know you know that's special. Though I don't think you realize *how* special just yet."

I open my mouth to protest, but then that brown book pops into my head.

Maybe she's right.

"Today, though, is even more special," she goes on. Once she's got a grip on the door handle, she turns to me. "You've held Great-Grampy JonJon's mitt. Now we're here to see his brother."

I stop dead. "Wait . . ."

Except I don't know what to say after that. Did I know Great-Grampy JonJon had a brother who's still alive? In theory, yes. I've heard Mom and Dad talk about some mysterious uncle when they're making grocery lists.

But said uncle was as real as the dusty old trunk I didn't think actually existed.

Here we go again.

She pulls the door open, and we step inside. "Uncle Jack is the sweetest man you'll ever meet. I've known him since your father and I started dating twenty-three years ago. Can't say he's always lucid, but he's still a delight."

"Umm. Okay."

The place is cozier than I expected: the lobby is full of comfy-looking couches, some of which have elderly people sitting on them knitting or reading. There's also a pair of older Black men at a small table in a corner, playing dominoes.

The security people we pass en route to the elevator bank all either wave or nod at Mama. She's clearly well known here. "You, umm . . . come here often?" I ask.

Elevator dings. "Often enough," she replies as we get on. It's just the two of us inside. "As I was saying, sometimes he's fully there. Aware of who he's talking to, and bright as sunshine. He's bursting with hilarious stories from his childhood with Great-Grampy JonJon, who was Jack's big brother and idol."

Still too much in shock about Uncle Jack being *alive* to respond.

We get off on the third floor, and go left down a long hallway. It's lined with framed paintings, and there's jazz music faintly floating through the air.

"But sometimes he's . . . in a different place," Mama continues. "Just sort of stares off into space and won't say much of anything." We stop in front of a door, and she isolates a key on her ring of nine thousand (no clue how she keeps up with which key goes to what lock). "All that to say I don't know which space he'll be in today," she says. "But your father and I agreed it's time for you to meet him." And then she opens the door.

"Uncle Jack?" she calls as we step inside.

It's . . . an apartment. The small entryway has a table with a purple orchid and a bowl on it. Mama drops her keys in the bowl.

"Millie? That you?"

Mama smiles. "Sure is. Brought someone I want you to meet."

"That so?" he says. "Well, come on in."

When we step into the living room, and I see the part-bald, medium-brown-skinned man sitting in a recliner—with a *Black Panther* comic book that looks real vintage open facedown on one of the chair arms—I can't help but smile, too. Old dude's got good reading taste.

Mama and I walk past his chair and sit side by side on the couch. Which is when he finally sees me. And as his surprisingly gray eyes lock onto my face, his wiry salt-and-pepper eyebrows shoot up toward the shiny spot at the center of his head where all the hair is gone. "Well, I'll be," he says.

"Uncle Jack, this is your great-grandniece."

He just stares.

"Her name is Shenice, and she's a fast-pitch soft-ball play—"

Mama's phone rings.

"Oh, shoot. I have to take this," she says, standing up. "Should be quick. You two chat while I'm gone."

And then she is. Gone.

Just like that.

Uncle Jack is still staring at me, but not saying a word. His storm-cloud-colored eyes give the eerie impression that he can see far more than what's actually in front of him.

It clicks, then: this is the other man in the framed picture I saw inside Great-Grampy JonJon's trunk.

"It's like he spit you out," Uncle Jack says, chopping through the silence in a way that makes me jump a bit.

"Huh?" Wait . . . gotta respect my elders. "Sorry, I'm not sure I understand what you mean, Uncle Jack."

"JonJon," he says. "You look just like him. Especially in them baseball clothes."

"Oh." Well, *that's* not creepy at all. "Umm . . . okay."

He's still staring. This is getting awkward. I turn toward the fireplace, even though the silence is making me itchy.

Where is Mama, and when is she coming back?

"He was framed, you know," Uncle Jack says then.

That sure grabs my attention. The brown leather book floats back to the top of my mind. "Framed?"

"He didn't do what they said he did," he replies, finally looking away. "I know he didn't."

46

My brain kicks into high gear, trying to figure out what to ask next. I know the word *framed* means a person was set up to look guilty of a crime they didn't commit. But what was he framed for?

What comes out: "How do you know he didn't do it, Uncle Jack?"

"'Cause I do. They thought I wouldn't notice, but I did."

When I don't respond, he looks at me again. "Nobody believed me, but I was telling the truth."

Now I'm the one who can't stop staring.

"I was tellin' it then, and I'm tellin' it now: *my* brother ain't no thief. He didn't do it." He faces forward again and *hmphs*.

Just as I open my mouth to speak, Uncle Jack says, "But I know who did."

6

Foul Ball

I'm able to *cheeeese!* my way through Mama's chat with Uncle Jack—which in comparison to mine was basically about nothing—the drive home, and dinner.

Daddy is beyond geeked that I was "really able to connect with" his favorite granduncle. "I know Jack can seem a few marbles short of a handful at times, but he's truly one of the kindest, wisest men I know," he says, heaping a softball-sized mound of mashed potatoes onto his plate. He adds a chunk of butter so big, it almost melts away my appetite.

"You're absolutely right about that," Mama chimes

in. "But, Vic, you *do* know those potatoes are already buttered, right?" The look of disgust on her face matches the one I'm trying to keep off of mine.

Daddy just grins and reaches for the chicken.

"Wait a minute," Drake says as though he's just waking up. "Did you say *marbles*? Like he actually *plays* marbles? I thought that was an old-people stereotype!"

"Not literal marbles, ya ding-dong," I say. "What Daddy means is that sometimes Uncle Jack isn't . . . all the way in touch with reality."

"With *our* reality, at least," Daddy corrects. "The one that belongs to him is just as valid."

"Your sister experienced that today and handled it swimmingly," Mama says, tossing a wink in my direction.

I drop my eyes to my plate. If only she knew.

"Soon we'll take *you* to meet Uncle Jack, Drake," Daddy says. "He's the last living Lockwood man in his generation, and you're the only one in yours."

"And *I* think you and Uncle Jack will connect because he, like you, was never interested in playing any type of 'batball,' as you call it," Mama adds.

"That's right!" Daddy says. "He was a numbers guy like you, son. Spent fifty years as an accountant."

"Well, that sounds boring," Drake replies. (Gotta love sixth graders.)

The conversation then shifts to chatter about my

team's district win, and discussion of our first section game—we Fulton Firebirds take on the Decatur Red Devils. And of course, good ol' Victor Lockwood can't resist a dad joke about how "hot" of a game it's going to be. "All I know is you girl bosses better bring them *FLAMES*, you feel me?" With a corny eyebrow dance.

It does distract me from my *other* distractions for a bit, and I'm able to knock out my homework and shower without getting sidetracked. But once I'm under my covers with the lights off, my mind starts to whirling like that one carnival ride that spins so fast, you get pinned to the wall on the inside.

And at the center of it all? The tale Uncle Jack told me during the fourteen minutes Mama was gone.

It was late '47. I was sixteen years old, which woulda made JonJon around twenty-four or twenty-five. He'd played in the Negro Southern League for three seasons. Joined shortly after he returned from a tour of duty overseas. I'll never forget him telling me that baseball helped him deal with the stuff he'd seen out on them battlefields.

I was riveted.

Anyhow, much as JonJon loved his team, he really wanted to go to the MLB. Not that he would've ever said it aloud, but I could tell he looked up to those fellas who'd gone over earlier in the year: Jackie Robinson and Larry Doby and Hank Thompson and Willard Brown. For weeks after each player made his debut, JonJon would talk nonstop about times he'd met each man, or games his team had played against theirs. He'd always end these trips down memory lane with a speech about how these boys going to the Majors was going to be the death of the Negro Leagues, but he wanted to play with them white boys, too. I could see it all over him.

It was all in his eyes. He wanted to be recruited real bad. And not just for the money: for the feeling of having proved his mettle, if you will. Hard as we tried to resist it in our family, wasn't no getting rid of that longing for approval from white folks. I knew he

wanted it. He was my big brother.
I could tell.

And my intuitions proved true!

At this, he shoved his finger in the air. Made me jump a little bit, won't lie. Though I didn't make a sound.

Because in November of that year, it came down through the grapevine that word of JonJon's .344 hitting average and lightning speed in the outfield had reached some scouts for a team that hadn't yet added a Negro to their roster.

And who could blame 'em for wanting JonJon Lee Lockwood, hmm? He was the best there was!

The more excited Uncle Jack got, the more I leaned in. Also, his use of the word *lightning* had given me a chill.

Wasn't nary other player better with a bat or quicker on his feet. It was darn near impossible to steal a base when he was at catcher. And when he was in the outfield, opposing batters used to try and avoid hitting the ball in his direction because they knew that if it wasn't a home run, Jumpin' JonJon would do just that: jump up and catch it.

Spring training kicked off and there they were: white recruiters. I knew exactly who they were because I was payin' close attention. I saw when they approached him after a game, and without him telling me a word, I knew—just knew—what the conversation had been about. Those same men showed up at the next three games, all of 'em whisperin' amongst themselves, and jotting things down in a little notebook.

Turns out, I wasn't the only one noticing. Next thing I know, word gets around that JonJon had been invited to some fancy benefit supper, and people are chattering because they're all *assuming the same thing: JonJon Lee Lockwood was gonna be the next Negro player to go to the Major Leagues.*

That's where it all went downhill.

And he stopped talking. Completely.

Almost like he had a sixth sense.

Because not two seconds later, Mama came back in.

Just when Uncle Jack had reached the good part.

I almost asked her to leave again. Almost told her that Jack and I were having a batball chat and needed a little more time. But when I opened my mouth, the old man cut me a warning look and gave his head a quick shake.

I felt like I was in some sort of spy movie.

Anyway, within a few minutes of Mama's return—she asked a series of seemingly well-rehearsed questions about nurses and medicines and joint pain and how he'd been feeling—we got up to leave. I had no idea what to say to Uncle Jack. *Hey, don't forget where you left off* felt mildly inappropriate, so I settled on a basic "Nice to meet you, sir."

Which is when I heard the thing that won't let me go:

"Ruined everything. Majors wouldn't take him, and he got booted from his Negro team and stripped of his records. They tried to blot him out like he'd never played at all. You gotta fix it," he said to the air in front of him.

Aka to me.

At least that's how it *felt*.

And despite having no idea how to "fix it"—or what *it* even is—I can't shake the feeling that he's right, and I need to do *something*.

So I toss and I turn. And when the house has been dead quiet for a while, I push the button on my clock that makes the time illuminate: 2:17 A.M.

I take a deep breath.

And then I do what I probably should've done days ago: I get out of my head and grab the skeleton key (more for comfort than anything) and my emergency flashlight, and I creep down the hall.

Quiet as I can be, I slip into PopPop's room and close myself in. Squeezing the skeleton key tight, I use the flashlight to locate the other door, and before I can think about it too much, I scurry up the stairs and flip the light on at the top.

Then I'm standing over the trunk. Which is wide open.

Key goes into the pocket, and then I reach down, quick as lightning, and grab the brown leather notebook that's been haunting my thoughts.

I'm about to jet back to my room as fast as I can—before somebody wakes up and catches me—but something else in the trunk grabs my eye.

A newspaper clipping, formerly hidden beneath the worn brown thing I came up here to take.

And now I can't pull my eyes away. So I reach down and grab it.

As I bring it to my face and read the headline, I gasp:

SCANDAL SEES "JUMPIN'" JONJON LEE LOCKWOOD OUSTED FROM ATLANTA BLACK CRACKERS AND NEGRO SOUTHERN LEAGUE

7

Strike Out

My backpack feels like it's full of bricks. Which probably sounds like an exaggeration, but the combination of Great-Grampy JonJon's brown book—that I have yet to open—that little newspaper clipping, and Daddy's ring, all of which are tucked down in the bag section that's designed to hold a laptop, makes me feel like the weight of the world is on my shoulders.

I also feel kinda silly about it. Especially considering that our first section tournament game is in two days. I should be *hyper*focused on softball right now. *And* I have a math test tomorrow I should get prepared for.

All that to say, *I* feel like quite the "ding-dong," as I like to call Drake when he's being *idiotic*, in the words of Britt-Marie. I have this amazing, momentous, historical thing going (hello, first all-Black team in a DYSA section tournament!), but I'm distracted by something that happened *seventy* years ago?

I can't shake it, though. This *scandal* the article mentions. I read that little piece of newspaper over a dozen times when I got back to my room last night. It was short. Told the story of a very important baseball glove that went missing from a silent charity auction. According to the article, it was donated by Joe DiMaggio and was "expected to fetch a fortune." (Who even talks like that?) But it disappeared at some point between the viewing/bidding and the reveal of the winners.

A witness claimed they saw Great-Grampy JonJon leaving the room where the auction items were being held while no one else was in there.

And that was enough. The article doesn't mention there being proof or if JonJon was arrested, but it *does* reiterate what the headline said: he was kicked out of his baseball league and stripped of the records he'd set.

Having read the thing, in a way I can understand why no one says much about Great-Grampy JonJon beyond the fact that he was a great baseball player. But after my time with Uncle Jack, I feel like it's possible that what *he* said is true: Great-Grampy JonJon *didn't* commit the crime that ended his career. Someone else did, and they pinned it on him.

Every time I reread the article, a new question formed.

Did anyone *find* this glove? And if so, where?

If Jack is telling the truth, and JonJon was innocent, did he fight the accusation?

And of course the loudest one: If JonJon didn't do it, who *did*?

This one bothers me the most. Because even if Uncle Jack does know and can tell me, would it matter? It was a super long time ago, and I'm sure *everyone* involved is . . . no longer alive.

So why can't I seem to let it go?

"Shenice!" Britt-Marie's voice yanks me back into the crazy-loud hallway of our middle school. She's practically running in my direction, looking like she just heard that every team we'll have to beat to win the league championship has forfeited. "Girl! You'll never believe it!"

Knowing the sort of thing Britt-Marie usually gets excited about, she's probably right. "What won't I believe this time?" I ask.

"Okay, so I made this bet with my grandpa—you know how old Black men swear they're right about *everything*?"

"Oh my god, Britt."

"*Goodness*," she corrects, Ms. Erica–style. "And it's *true*. Anyway, he was *sure* he knew more baseball trivia than me. So I told him we could pull up a game on the internet, and if I could answer more questions correctly than he could, he'd have to buy me that mad expensive Louisville Slugger LXT bat ol' girl with the glistening gold tresses had at that Sharks game. You remember?"

How could I forget? "Of course."

"Yeah, well . . . homeboy lost."

I snort. "Did you just call your grandfather *homeboy*?"

"I mean, good old Grampy tries to act all cool and hip, so . . ." She shrugs. "Bottom line: new bat for me. And just in time, right?" She nudges me with her elbow.

But my mind has already drifted off. Especially at the mention of the word *Grampy*. "Just in time for what?"

She stops dead. In the middle of the hallway. "You're not for real."

"What?"

"The *captain* of my fast-pitch softball team did *not* just imply that our first section tournament game is something she put on the back burner of her brain. She didn't. I *know* she didn't. . . ."

Whoops!

"Relax, Britt. I know we have a game."

"Well, I would hope so!"

The first bell rings, saving me.

"Dang it," I say. "I needed to get to Bonner's early to ask about . . . that last assignment he gave us! Gotta run!"

"Tell him I said hiiiii!"

Britt-Marie has a raging crush on our English teacher. It's gross. "He's too old for you!" I toss over my shoulder as I scurry off.

I can hear her laughter behind me.

Unfortunately, my lie to Britt about needing to talk to him aside, Mr. Bonner isn't the least bit helpful *this* morning: in our continued study of the book *Monster*, today's lesson is about truth-seeking. It hits me: we're reading a book about a main character who's on trial for a crime he claims he didn't commit.

Wild.

"So what methods of truth-seeking are employed in Steve's narrative? Mr. Lamar?"

Mr. Bonner is notorious for calling on people instead of waiting for someone to volunteer an answer. And the student he called on—William "Scoob" Lamar—is caught completely off guard. "Sir?" he says.

Mr. Bonner smirks. "Mm-hmm. Quit doodling during my lesson. I asked what methods of truth-seeking you noticed in the narrative."

"Oh," Scoob says, sliding right back into class as if he hasn't missed a beat. "Well, it reads to me like there's a heavy reliance on eyewitnesses—"

He can say that again.

And as hard as I try to catch the rest of what Scoob says, that *eyewitness* who claimed to see my great-grandfather come out of that auction—and the career-ruining results of those claims—take over my brain. Despite being blanked out for the rest of the lesson, I find myself approaching Mr. Bonner's desk after class.

"'Sup, Superstar?" he says with a smile. It's like the light *dings* off his perfect teeth.

I roll my eyes, Britt-Marie's crush shoving its way to the front of my mind. She'd totally give the thumb of her throwing hand to hear those words spoken to *her.* "Bet you say that to *all* the students," I reply before I can think better of it.

Thankfully, he just laughs. "Nope. Only the ones I believe it to be true of. What can I do for you, Miss Lockwood?"

Now I gulp. "Well . . . about this whole truth-seeking thing," I begin.

And end. Because I don't really know what to say next.

"Yes? About that . . . what?"

"Umm . . ."

Swallow again.

"Well, say a person *wanted* to seek out some truth, but wasn't exactly sure where to start?" Man, I feel so silly right now. Should've planned this out or something.

"Mm-hmm. And what sort of truth is this person seeking out?"

"Well, that's what she—I mean, *they* aren't completely sure of."

He smirks.

I hate it.

"What makes *them* think there's truth that needs to be sought out?" he asks.

Now I sigh. "Well, a family member started telling them this *story*. But they didn't get to finish because a *different* family member came into the room. When they—the truth-seeker, I mean—got home, they wanted to find out more, so they went digging and came up with this . . . I guess it would be a primary source. It's a newspaper clipping that confirms at least some of what the storytelling family member was saying. And now . . . I guess the person wants to know the rest. Of the truth."

He slow-nods, and I hold my breath. Hoping to the heavens that he won't ask why. Because I don't have an answer for that.

"Do any other family members know the rest of this story? They'd be secondary sources, obviously. . . ." He winks. "But they could potentially help point the truth-seeker in the right direction."

"I don't know," I say honestly.

It's not that I haven't considered telling Daddy Uncle Jack's story, and asking if he knows anything. But I can't bring myself to do it. Every time I think about it, I hear the final words the old man said: *"You gotta fix it."* No, he wasn't talking *to* me in the sense of looking me in the eye . . . but I'm pretty sure the "you" he was referring to is *me*. As in Shenice Ashley "Lightning" Lockwood.

"Well," Mr. Bonner goes on, "if *the person* feels as though they have enough information—names, dates, access to primary sources like newspapers and photographs—they can seek out some truth that way."

I nod. "Okay."

"Trip to the library might prove useful."

No idea why I didn't think of that. "True. Thanks, Mr. Bonner."

"No problem."

I give a dorky little wave and head to the door.

"One other thing, Miss Lockwood," he says just before I step out.

I pause and look back at him.

"Deliver this message to the truth-seeker specifically from me." He leans back in his chair. "Unless the story-teller has passed, the easiest way to find out more is to just . . . go ask them."

He shrugs and raises his palms like he just said the simplest yet most brilliant thing in the world.

If only he knew.

8

Bases Loaded

As if there isn't *more* than enough on my mind by the time we get to the ballpark for our first section game, the moment I step out of the Firebus, I look across the parking lot and spot someone I hoped to never see again.

I stop dead, and Britt-Marie crashes right into me.

"Geez, Lockwood," she says.

And I guess she notices the look on my face because her next words are "Why do you look like you just saw Medusa and turned to stone?"

I don't respond. Just keep staring.

"Sheniiiiice?" And she taps me on the shoulder.

Still can't move.

"Lightning? O captain, our captain? What gives?"

She must follow my eyes then. Because the next words out of her mouth are: "Oh, sugar honey iced tea."

"Yeah" is all I can muster.

"Wait a minute, is that . . ." Laury, our queen of first base, steps up beside us. "No way."

"Way," I say.

Then, almost as though she can feel our stares, the girl's head turns, and she sees me.

Her face lights up like it's Christmas.

"Sugar honey iced tea is right," I say.

My final year playing slow pitch, I was nine. Fourth grade. I was the only Black girl on the team, and three games into the season, we had a match against the Birchville Bruisers.

Which should've been warning enough. Because that's exactly what these players were.

Everyone on their team was bigger—in height *and* weight—than everyone on ours. To the point where our coach wondered aloud if they were actually eligible for the ten-and-under league. And they played rough and dirty. Threw faster and swung harder than any players our crew had ever seen. They were quick on their feet, stole every stealable base at least once, and were clearly out for blood.

Bottom of the sixth, they're up to bat. Two outs, two

strikes, one of which was a foul ball. They had a runner on first—blond with wispy hair she couldn't seem to keep out of her mouth or eyes despite it being in a braid. And a runner on third. We'll call her B-Cubed: Bloody Bruising Becca. She was half a head taller than me and much bigger. Hair was dyed bright blue, and she had a pale face with bright red cheeks.

She genuinely *looked* mean.

The whole thing happened super fast: B-Cubed shifted her stance in a way that let me know she planned to steal home the moment the ball was released. I had just switched over to catcher from second base—partially because my coach realized I *noticed* stuff like a shifted stance—and I was still getting my bearings. But as our pitcher prepped to toss, I started really sweating.

As soon as the ball was in the air, B-Cubed took off in my direction. And as I mentioned, this was *slow* pitch. So even if the batter swung and the ball wound up in my mitt, I wouldn't have been able to get it to our third-base girl fast enough for her to tag B-Cubed out.

The batter managed a grounder and got to running, but (luckily) our shortstop scooped it up and fired it to first base, where the girl was quickly tagged out.

But my few seconds of distraction cost me big: next thing I knew, B-Cubed was flying at me . . . and sinking into a slide.

I planted my feet in case the ball suddenly came my way. I was looking toward first for it when I felt pain in my leg beyond anything I'd ever experienced.

And then I was on the ground. Screaming.

B-Cubed had slid right into my ankle . . . with her very much *illegal*-in-our-league metal cleats. Ripped through my tall socks and took out two large (for a nine-year-old, at least) chunks of my flesh. There was blood everywhere.

And my ankle was fractured in three places.

To this day, I'm convinced she did it on purpose. For one, I was deliberately standing *behind* home plate. Her path was 100 percent clear. Also, the smirk on her face when we made eye contact as I was carried off the field said it all.

But I couldn't actually *say* that. Even at nine, I knew being the only speck of brown on the field was a lot. Being the sole speck of brown *and* accusing an opposing (all-white) team member of foul play?

Definitely a no-go.

She had to sit out five games for the cleat violation. *I* was out for the entire season.

And the incident became a thing of legend among the smattering of Black softball players across our city. To the point that when I showed up to Coach Nat's first recruitment meeting for the Firebirds, seven out of the thirteen other girls who were there knew who I was.

"Unreal," Cortlin (left field) says as she joins the staring circle.

B-Cubed has bright red hair now instead of blue. And is a Roswell Red Devil.

Fitting.

Britt-Marie turns to me. Thankfully, every member of *my* team *does* believe Rebecca Murphy slid into my ankle on purpose. Britt looks scared.

But Laury steps in front of me and puts both hands on my shoulders. "Shake it off, Lockwood. That was three years ago," she says, practically reading my mind. "You are the *lightning* of this team now, and ain't no apple-haired she-devil gonna knock you off your square, ya dig?" (Every time Mama hears Laury talk, she says, "I swear that girl hopped straight outta the 1970s.")

"Yeah," I say. "I dig."

But I definitely don't "dig." And it shows for the duration of all six excruciating innings.

Thanks to the presence of B-Cubed—who eyeballs me the whole time, no lie—and the constant fielding-glove reminders of my great-grandfather's supposed theft, I spend most of the game surely looking like I'm afraid of the dang ball. I have more drops than in every other match of the season combined. I miss an out because I throw too wide when one of the Red Devils tries to steal second (she succeeds). I completely miss one of Cala's pitches because I mix up the fastball and changeup signals . . . which gives the Red Devil on third base the perfect opportunity to steal home.

And she does.

Putting them up one run at the top of the final inning.

My head is in the flames, all right. The flames of the place where Red Devils are said to come from.

Thankfully, every *other* Firebird has their act together, and we manage three additional runs, winning the game. But, wow, is the ride home awkward. Nobody's really celebrating because it got so close at the end. I'm sure everyone assumes B-Cubed's presence got to me (and they're not wrong), so nobody asks any questions. But *that* just makes things next-level uncomfortable. Like a big rhino sitting in the van with us.

Wouldn't a *good* captain have brushed B-Cubed off and assured her team that they had everything they needed to win? And maybe that's what *would've* happened had I not spent so much time over the past few days thinking about my dead great-grandpa. I have to get back on track.

If I think my teammates' silence in the Firebus means I won't have to talk about anything, I'm wrong. Because when Daddy and I pull into the driveway, there's a person sitting on our porch steps. Gazing *all forlornly,* as Britt-Marie would say, at the gray house next door.

It makes me smile—Scoob's presence is always a ray of sunshine—but also makes me a little sad: that house he's staring at used to be his grandmother's. And it was turquoise until the new people moved in and painted it a year ago.

"Catch," I say, grabbing his attention before I pretend to throw a ball at him. He hollers and ducks, and I laugh. Scoob definitely prefers computer coding to anything sports-related.

"Oh, so you're a comedian now?" he says, climbing to his feet. He grew over the past year and is now a few inches taller than me. Lately, he does this thing where he looks down over the tip of his nose at me, and one corner of his mouth ticks up. It sometimes makes me feel a little . . .

Nah. Never mind. Moving on.

"Tough game," he says. "Glad you won. But *whew.*"

"You can say that again." I drop my stuff in the grass and plop down on the second step. "Thrilled you came, but also *not.* That was the worst game I've ever played." I stare out across the street and shake my head. "And you were there to witness it."

He takes a seat beside me. "I still think you're the greatest," he says. And he bumps me with his shoulder.

My face gets warm, and I swallow instead of speaking.

"So, umm . . ." Now he seems nervous. Which makes *me* nervous. What if he, like . . . asks me to marry him or something? An eighth grader proposed to Britt-Marie just last week.

"Yeah?" I say, trying to urge him along. (Do I maybe *want* him to ask me to marry him?)

"Okay, don't take this the wrong way, or think I'm stalking you or something. But you've been sorta *off* this week," he says. "Is everything okay?"

Oh.

"Ummm . . ." I stare at my chipped orange nail polish. (And, yes, Britt-Marie was appalled when she noticed it this afternoon.)

"No pressure to tell me anything, obviously," Scoob continues. "I guess I just . . . wanted you to know I'm here for you. If you *do* want to talk about something." Now he's looking at *his* hands, which are clasped between his knees.

I peek at his face. His big eyes and chubby cheeks have morphed into something . . . different. Something, dare I say, *cute.*

Like *really* cute.

Super don't need *this*—swoopy, fluttery stomach thing when I look at my best boy friend (UGH!)—on top of everything else right now.

But then he turns to me. And I don't know what it

is, but the next thing I know, I'm taking a deep breath, and spilling.

Like . . . everything.

From the trip through PopPop's room ("Wait, you went *in* there?") to the discovery of the actual trunk ("Wait, it's *REAL?*"). From the mitt to the brown book. The dreams, the distraction, the visit to Uncle Jack, the article.

"And now I have no idea what to do," I say. "I played *terribly* tonight, Scoob. And yes, seeing that Bruiser Devil—"

Scoob snorts.

"I'm serious! Facing that ankle breaker wasn't great, *William.*"

"Sorry, sorry." But of course he doesn't stop laughing. Which, fine, makes me laugh, too.

See? Sunshine.

"Anyway, homegirl definitely threw me off. But even if she *hadn't* been there, I probably would've still played horribly because of all the *other* stuff on my mind, you know?"

"Makes sense," he says.

"I just . . . don't know what to do. Part of me wants to drop the whole JonJon thing. It happened forever ago, and for all I know, the next time I see Uncle Jack, he'll have forgotten about it or something."

"Watch that ageism and ableism, young lady," Scoob

says with a wink. "Elderly people can be way more with it than you'd think."

"Yeah, I hear you," I say. "But that doesn't really help me."

"So do something that will."

It makes my heart beat faster. Because I'm pretty sure I already know what he's thinking. "Like what?"

"Well, let's get honest: Guessing you haven't opened the brown book?"

"I can't do it," I say, shaking my head. "Feels too sacred."

"Understood. And you haven't told anybody but me about this whole thing, right? So there's really no pressure to figure anything out. *Can* you drop it?"

I huff. "I think we both know the answer to that, Scoob."

"That's what I thought. So then you know what you gotta do."

He's right. I do know.

Still, I would rather hear him say it. "*Do* I know?"

He shoots me a dose of side-eye that makes my palms go damp. (Which is actually kind of nasty. *Why* are people so gaga about the whole "crush" thing again?) "Yes. You do," he says.

"Will you just tell me?" I nudge him with my elbow, and he shakes his head.

"Fine," he says. "You gotta talk to your uncle Jack."

9

Swing, Batter Batter

Thinking about it now, there was no reason for me to be nervous about asking Mama and Daddy if I could visit Uncle Jack again. I should've assumed from how excited they were the *first* time I met him that they'd not only agree, but would be geeked that I want to go back.

Because they are.

"Oh, oh, *oh*, Uncle Jack is gonna be so *tickled*!" Daddy says, *giddy as a gumdrop* (something else he sometimes says when excited). "And *you* taking advantage of the chance to connect with the last living Lockwood elder . . . I'm just so *proud*!"

Thing is: I was so worried about the parentals poten-tially giving me the third degree, I didn't consider that Uncle Jack might be having one of his . . . less *lucid* days when I came to see him again.

And unfortunately he is.

"You ever notice how when you start a fire, the mem-ory of exactly how it burned stays with you lonnnnnnng after you extinguish it?" he says, staring through the win-dow. I've been here for twenty minutes, and everything he's said has been along these lines. I'm trying to hold it together and stay patient, but I'm getting desperate. It was extra hot today, and practice was brutal—lots of fielding relays, fence sprints, and of course, push-ups—so I'm exhausted. And I'm running out of time. Mama will be back in precisely thirty-eight minutes, and if things continue the way they've been going, this visit will have been a total waste.

Which probably isn't a very nice thing to say, but it's how I feel in *this* moment.

I decide to try a different tactic. "You're so right about the fire thing, Uncle Jack," I say. "Hey, did you know my softball team is named the Firebirds? A few days ago, we won the first round of our section tourna-ment against a team called the Red Devils. How's that for *hot*?"

"You know what's *really* hot?" he replies. "Habanero peppers. Wheeeew-wheeeeeee, one time I ate me one of them at a Mexican restaurant in Virginia, and I thought my tongue was gonna shrivel up and turn to ash!"

"Wow!" I slouch down deeper into his living room couch.

Maybe I *should* just let this whole thing go. I've read that newspaper clipping from the trunk more often that I can count, and spent time at the public library in the archive of "periodicals"—such a strange word. I now know that the article was printed in a small Black American–run paper called the *Atlanta Bulletin*. But it's the only mention I was able to find of Great-Grampy JonJon's whole "scandal."

There's also nothing about the incident on the internet. Which kinda freaked me out: If you can't find information about a thing on the *internet*, is said thing even real?

Something else I couldn't find: complete Negro League team rosters. There are websites that mention a handful of names—usually just the "top players"—but none with year-by-year lists of who was on the team.

Of course, I had no problem finding multiple minor-league white team lineups from the same years.

I know Great-Grampy JonJon was on a Negro Southern League team because of all the trophies and plaques in our attic shrine. But it's bothering me to no end that I can't find *evidence* of his participation in the place that's supposed to have *all* the answers to *everything*.

Like what other pieces of history just . . . aren't there anymore?

"You all right over there, Millie?"

"Oh, ummm . . ." Do I correct a dude who's more than ninety years old? "I'm actually Millie's daughter, Shenice," I say. "Millie stepped out but will be back in about half an hour."

He doesn't respond.

Uh-oh. "Did you hear me, Uncle Jack? Sorry if I overstepped. I just didn't want you thinking I'm Millie when I'm not—"

"I know who you are," he says.

Instantly, it's like the temperature in the room has changed. Though I can't say whether it feels hotter or colder—I just know the air feels different.

"Jacob Carlyle," he says next.

"Huh?"

"That was his name. The fella who set JonJon up."

I sit up straight but try to keep my cool. Don't wanna do anything that will throw him back off.

But I have to keep him talking. "Will you tell me what happened?"

"Where'd I leave off last time?" he says.

I'm shocked. "Umm . . ." *Where* did *he leave off?* "Something about a dinner and things . . . going downhill?"

He nods once, and I exhale the most relieved breath of my life. "Sounds about right."

He stops again.

This is so nerve-racking.

"What exactly went downhill, if you don't mind my asking?" I say.

"Well, everything, really," Jack replies. "He went to that fancy supper with all them white folks even though I told him not to. He didn't listen to me because I was young, you see. Only sixteen. But I knew something bad would happen if he went. And it did."

"Do you know exactly *what* happened?"

"Exactly? No. I wasn't there. But what I do know is this . . ."

I lean forward.

"What JonJon told *me*—but wouldn't tell the authorities— is that he'd gotten turned around in that big old house."

"Old house?" I ask before I can catch myself.

"Where this *supper* was held. It was some rich man's mansion down at the southern edge of the city. JonJon showed me the photograph that was on the invitation. Place wasn't nothing but a gussied-up plantation house."

"Got it," I say, wanting to move things along. Only twenty-four minutes until Mama comes back. "And Jon-Jon got lost inside the house?"

"That's what he said," Jack replies. "Was looking for the washroom and took a wrong turn. Between the two of us, I was surprised to hear they permitted JonJon to move anywhere in that place without an escort. People's ideas about Negroes were far worse back then than they are now, you see. Guess them folks were really trying to show him they believed in equality."

"Huh," I reply. "That's awful and yet makes perfect sense."

Jack nods. "JonJon said someone told him where the washroom was, but instead he wound up in the room with all the valuables in it. The items that were up for auction."

That fits with what the article says.

"He hightailed it out of there, but didn't manage to exit unseen. There was a man there, a minor-league ball-player named Jacob Carlyle. He was the one who came forward as the witness."

"Ah, okay."

"He's also the one who stole that glove."

Whoa.

"How do you know?"

"I saw him with it."

Umm . . . "You did?"

"Mm-hmm. His minor team and JonJon's Negro team shared a stadium. And I was a batboy there. I was headed out after a Negro game, and I happened to overhear some of the minor team players chattering on their way in. One of them—Jacob Carlyle, which I knew because I'd seen the tail end of his games countless times—was trying to convince the others that the glove he was wearing had belonged to Joe DiMaggio. But they all just laughed at him. Wouldn't believe a word he said."

"I probably wouldn't have believed him, either."

"Neither would I, if I hadn't known that the glove had gone missing. I *knew* JonJon hadn't taken it, and that Carlyle had been the witness who said he'd seen Jon-Jon leaving that room. Him suddenly telling his buddies he had the glove seemed too suspect to be coincidence. Ain't hard to put them pieces together."

He certainly has a point. "Okay, so what happened next?"

"Well, I waited for his game to end, and then I followed him out. Had to sit in a different part of the bus at that point—Negroes in the back—so he was none the wiser to my presence. I watched him, though. And he was mad. Flashing that glove hadn't gotten him the response he wanted."

Guy sounds like a *real piece of work*, as Daddy would put it.

"I kept my eye on him over the next few weeks as the fire came down on JonJon. And *I* was mad. Heard him laughing about JonJon's demise at the stadium one day. Told some teammates, 'Them Black boys shouldn't be allowed in the Major League at all, let alone be given the spots *we're* working hard for.' He'd been envious of JonJon, and he wanted to ruin him. I'm certain of it."

I've never felt anything like the white-hot rage now churning inside my stomach over the fact that this *Jacob* guy succeeded in his stupid, life-breaking mission.

"So what happened to the glove, do you think?"

"Oh, I know exactly what happened to it. That Jacob Carlyle blew his knee out trying to steal third base during a game a few weeks later. Ended his career."

"Served him right, if you ask me." I *hmph*.

That makes Uncle Jack laugh. It's one of the most delightful sounds I've ever heard. "I like your style, gal," he says.

Which makes *me* burst into a fit of giggles. I *really* like Uncle Jack.

"But I saw him a few months after. He stumbled onto a city bus, stone drunk and mumbling, and some other white man recognized him. I was only a couple of rows behind where he plopped himself down beside the guy, so I heard him ramblin' about how he'd packed up all his baseball equipment and dropped it off at the stadium's lost-and-found. 'Including that damned DiMaggio glove,' he said. Claimed the thing was 'cursed.'"

My heart starts beating faster.

"I slipped in there after I finished my next shift— Negroes weren't allowed in certain parts of the stadium, but the security fella, Joe, let me in. He was always kind to me, that Joe."

And he stops again. (Gah!)

"So? Did you find it?"

He nods once. "Sure did."

"And . . . ?" Can't breathe now. "What'd you do with it? Did you turn it in?"

"Couldn't've. That woulda made JonJon look guilty, his brother suddenly turning up with the contraband. No one was gonna take the word of a Negro batboy over that of a white man."

I hate that he's right. And that I feel like I know it from experience. (Broken ankle from illegal cleat, anyone?) "I guess that's true," I say.

"It is. So instead I took that, one of Carlyle's caps with his name in it, and a photograph of him and two teammates, wrapped it all up tight, and stashed 'em somewhere safe."

And now I have a *bunch* of questions crashing around in my head and don't know which one to ask first. Where did he hide it? Has he told anyone else? Did he ever go back for it?

I open my mouth to start with the first one and—

"Knock, knock!" Mama says, coming in. (Okay, but why even *bother* to knock?) "You all have a good visit?"

"Mm-hmm," Uncle Jack says. "I was just telling the young lady here about the house me and JonJon grew up in. We moved there when I was two years old, shortly after it was built. He and I used to play hide-and-go-seek, and this one time, I discovered a loose floorboard beneath my bed. So I got me a little chest from my mama, and I hid it underneath and started puttin' all my personal treasures in it. Hell, I bet my old stuffed bunny rabbit is still in there. Mr. Floppers was his name. . . ."

And just like that, he's gone again.

10

Safe

It doesn't smack me until the middle of the night three days later, but once it does—and I jolt out of sleep— I feel like the world's *biggest* ding-dong: That whole loose floorboard story? Uncle Jack was telling me where he hid the glove.

He *had* to be. Just like the last time Mama walked in on a Very Important Conversation and he said something seemingly random as we were leaving that actually wasn't random at all.

Which means I have a real lead on this thing.

But also . . . I don't know if it matters. I'm no math whiz—hate the subject with the passion of a Firebird, if you want the truth—but I *can* handle basic subtraction. If Uncle Jack was sixteen in 1947, he was born in 1931. Beyond the fact that this means he is reaaaaally old, if they moved into the house when he was two, and the house was new then, that would mean it was built in . . . 1933.

That's almost ninety years ago.

Ninety.

Do houses even last that long?

I lie awake, staring at the ceiling, trying to figure out why I care about this enough to let it disturb my Very Important Sleep (we have a *game* tomorrow and *double* practice the day after, for "goodness" sake). Chances are, that house—and the Joe DiMaggio glove that caught and killed my great-grandfather's baseball career—is long gone.

And even if they *aren't*, what difference would it make? Great-Grampy JonJon passed away when Daddy was a *kid*. There's obviously no clearing his name so he can play again. And Jacob Carlyle . . . if he *is* still alive, and I could prove he set JonJon up, I doubt anybody would throw a dude that old in jail.

Uncle Jack said I "gotta fix it." But what exactly am I supposed to *fix*?

I have to let this go. We have a championship to get to. And win. Great-Grampy JonJon's chance at making history might've been stolen from him. Squandering mine—and my team's—because I'm distracted isn't an option.

What I *gotta* do is be a good captain so we can win our games.

I flip over onto my stomach and shove my arms beneath my pillow to get more comfortable. But when I do, something falls to the floor with a *thunk*. Scares the bejeebus outta me. So I turn on the lamp attached to my headboard and cautiously peek over the edge of the bed.

It's the brown book. Which I still haven't opened. In fact, every time I touch it, I'm careful to avoid the leather strings.

Totally forgot I put it under my pillow.

I can't bring myself to even pick it up right now. Almost feels like if I do, it'll burn me or something. Like now that I have all this *information*—which really doesn't feel like much information at all—the spirit of my ancestor that's trapped in the journal isn't going to let me rest until I avenge him.

Maybe Britt-Marie is right about me watching too many wizard movies . . .

I roll onto my side and sigh. Look at the clock: 3:24 A.M.

Our quarterfinals match of the section tournament is in six hours and thirty-six minutes (there's that good math again).

I can't do anything about Great-Grampy JonJon or Uncle Jack right now.

So I shut my eyes and try to get some rest.

When I *do* manage to actually fall asleep? En route to the game.

It's an hour-and-a-half drive to the little country town where we'll face off against the Midville Mighty Ducks. (*That's* a mascot for you.) And within ten minutes of hitting the highway, I'm down for the count.

I wake to disco-loving Laury's phone in my face. On the screen is an image of *me*, knocked out, mouth open, drool running. Laury, Cala, and Hennessey are all facing me, with Khyler on my left and Britt-Marie on my right, trapping me in a circle of ridicule.

Laury is grinning. "Good nap, Slick?"

The other girls laugh.

"I hate you all," I reply.

"Let's not use the H-word, ladies," Ms. Erica says from the front seat. I swear that woman has supersonic hearing. "We must *edify*!"

I shut my eyes so I can roll them without anybody seeing (and tattling like a six-year-old). "Yes, Ms. Erica," we all say as one.

"Okay, everybody out!" from Coach Nat. "We've got some duck butt to set on fire!"

Britt-Marie snorts. "Coach, you are *clearly* taking those 'suburban dad' aspirations pretty seriously with jokes like that."

"Zip it and get outta my van, Hogan."

We all laugh. Which feels pretty good.

The good feels don't last, though. As we exit and make our way to the playing field, it becomes pretty apparent that this maybe isn't friendly territory for a team like ours. Moments like these, I want to check a calendar to see what century we're in. Certainly doesn't feel like the twenty-first.

"Sheesh, do they know the Confederacy *lost* the war?" from Britt-Marie (of course).

"Will you shush?" I say. "This is *not* the time!"

Because in addition to the parking lot full of vehicles with Confederate flag emblems on them, the *looks* coming at us from the people said vehicles belong to? Yeah, this feels *far* worse than the evil eye B-Cubed threw my way after ending my season three years ago.

And it's not just me.

"Hey, Captain Lightning?" Cala says under her breath as she steps into stride beside me. She links her arm with mine. "I don't like how those people are eyeballing us."

"Me neither, Quickfire," I reply.

By the time our feet touch the field, it's clear that we're *all* feeling . . . off.

And I have no idea what to say.

There's a nervousness that runs through our warm-up. Some dropped balls here and there, and nobody throwing or running as confidently as usual. Before the game begins, Coach Nat and Ms. Erica pull us into a huddle inside the dugout instead of on the field.

And Coach's pep talk is . . . different. I'm pretty sure we can all feel *her* discomfort. "Uhhh . . . so this is . . . umm . . ." She looks at her feet, and me and my teammates all peek at each other. The last time Coach Nat couldn't find words was after Hennessey's dad passed away last season.

This is no good.

"Okay, listen to me, sweet babies," Ms. Erica says, jumping in. And we all turn to her. "All of you are old enough to know—and have probably felt—that the world ain't always a nice or fair place for bright and bold young royals like you. But that is *exactly* what you are— royalty—and me and Nat want you to get out there and show those bigots who's boss."

Coach Nat smacks her own forehead. "Babe."

"Well, it's true, isn't it?"

Coach stares out at the visitor stands for a few seconds and takes a deep breath. Then she nods. "Okay. How many of you were thrown off by the Confederate flags?"

We glance around at each other, and all slowly lift our hands.

"Do you know why?"

"I mean . . . it's the most well-known symbol of the governing body in this country that supported the continuation of US chattel slavery," Britt-Marie says. (And no one is surprised.)

"Which in plain English means they didn't want Black people to be freed. Ever." From Laury. "Right?"

"Yep," Ms. Erica replies.

"And how does seeing it *now* make you feel?" Coach Nat asks.

"Unsafe," Laury says.

"Hated," from Hennessey.

"Like there's something wrong with me," Cala chimes in.

Ms. Erica's face is so red with rage, I worry she's going to morph into an *actual* firebird.

"And is there any supporting evidence for that? The idea that there's something wrong with you?" Coach Nat goes on.

Cala takes in all of our faces. "Well . . . no. Not really."

"True," Laury says, doing the same. "In fact, I think we're pretty solid in the *cool* department."

Coach Nat smiles. "And do you suck at fast-pitch softball?"

"What?" Hennessey says. "*Heavens* no."

Britt-Marie examines her nails . . . which means she's about to say something "fresh," as Mama likes to call it. "I mean, we're *clearly* the best team in our district. And also better than at least one team in this section. Wouldn't be here if we weren't."

"*Exactly,*" Coach Nat says.

I (finally) feel some fire bubble up inside me. "So if we know there's nothing wrong with us, *and* we're good at this game . . ." I stick my hand out in front of me. Slowly but surely, my teammates' hands land on top of mine, and I can feel the air shift.

Feels *real* good. Better than the laughter, even.

"What do you think we should do, Firebirds?" I say, loud enough for the whole field to hear me.

"Blaze UP!" everyone replies.

"Huh?"

"BLAZE UP!" they shout again.

"Can't hear you!"

"*BLAZE UP!*"

And we lift our hands into the air.

11

Off Base

Not only do we roast the Mighty Ducks and eat them for lunch *and* dinner—final score: 9 to 1— but I play the best game I have in *multiple* seasons: four for four, with two doubles and three RBIs, and I threw not one, but *two* people out, including a player who was trying to steal third.

And it feels great to win—and advance to the semi-finals. Especially as *us*, in an unwelcoming space like that one.

But over the next few days, there's an itchy feeling inside me that I can't seem to shake loose.

While I've definitely seen Confederate flags before

and had a general idea of what they represent, that game was my first time actually interacting with the *people* who, like . . . deliberately put that symbol on their stuff.

The confusing part is . . . they weren't what I expected. Yes, there was a handful of Duck fans who really did give us dirty looks throughout the game. And there was a point when I was coming around third that I swear I heard a slur used in the Duck stands. (I'm sure us kicking their team's butt didn't help them like us more.)

But where I was bracing myself for things like having the N-word shouted at me when I was up to bat, or having an ump make bad calls because he didn't want us to win? None of that happened. In fact, there was one guy who called out a compliment a couple of times. Like when Khyler *almost* hit a home run (she wound up on third), I heard him say, "Wowee, what a zinger! That little gal can *hit*."

I'm thankful, in a way, that what I assumed would happen based on that flag symbol didn't really happen at all. But in light of the *other* stuff on my mind—aka the story of a white man tanking my great-grandpa's career because he was jealous . . . and because he could—I'm almost certain that even now, over seventy years later, it could've gone worse for us in a setting like that.

All I know is that after seeing those flags and feeling like all my power and the *good* things about me had been instantly snatched away, I think I understand why

Uncle Jack didn't go to the authorities with that glove. The strangest part is that while I'm thrilled we won, it also made me afraid: Great-Grampy JonJon being *good* at something inspired a person who didn't like it—and who had more power than he did—to do an awful thing. The Mighty Ducks *seemed* to take their loss in stride, but what if they hadn't? They could totally still call the league *now* and say that we cheated or something.

I have no idea what would happen if they did, and I hope to never find out. But knowing we won fair and square because we were the better team isn't the least bit comforting. As Ms. Erica said, *the world ain't always a nice or fair place* for people like me and my teammates.

It wasn't for my great-grandfather. Or my uncle Jack. Or my PopPop.

And I hate it.

Things take a turn for the even more bizarre a few days later.

Starts at practice. We're running some batting drills with Coach Nat on the mound and Ms. Erica shouting encouragement from just beyond the foul line, when this awful, nasally voice rings out near third base:

"That ain't how you hit no baseball!"

Catches us ALL off guard, but especially me: during this rotation, I'm *at* third base. I literally jump and whip around. And there on the other side of the fence is a pair of boys, both pale-skinned and red-cheeked. One is long and scrawny like somebody grabbed his greasy brown hair and pulled up to stretch him out. The other? Squat and round and in a backward ball cap so tight, it might be cutting off circulation to his brain.

Basically a human softball and bat. Standing together.

"You chicks are trash," the short, dumpy one says.

I put my ungloved hand on my hip. "Excuse me?"

"I didn't stutter," the ruddy-faced bat says. "I said: That. Ain't. How. You hit. No baseball."

"Well, you're right about that, ding-a-ling," says a voice from right behind me. I turn, and there's Britt-Marie. Arms crossed.

I smile. These dum-dums are *really* in trouble now.

"Your use of a double negative actually *works* here," she continues. "Because we 'ain't' trying to hit 'no baseball.' Those round yellow things are called *softballs*. And *you* couldn't hit one if it was sitting on a tee."

"Ladies, ignore them," Coach Nat says. But I'm pretty sure it's just a formality. There's *zero* force behind the command. We all know that once Britt-Marie gets going, there's no stopping her until she's finished. I peek over my shoulder, and sure enough, Coach has left the mound and is headed toward the dugout.

Of note: this isn't the first time some knucklehead

boys have interrupted our practice with their "toxically masculine tomfoolery," as Britt-Marie puts it. No clue why some boys can't handle the idea of *non*-boys being good at anything athletic, but last time it was a group of five slightly younger baseballers—in uniform—and Britt-Marie told them off so bad, two of them burst into tears.

"Ah, so you're the mouthy one," the bat says, grinning like the Cheshire Cat from *Alice in Wonderland*. (Creep.) "I remember you."

The ball nods. "Mm-hmm. Me too."

"Remember me?" Britt-Marie says, more annoyed than taken aback.

"Yup," says the bat. "Y'all think you're so good just 'cause you beat the Mighty Ducks on Saturday. But you had to have cheated because we been watching you practice, and y'all don't even swing good."

What the . . . "What do *you* know about our game against the Ducks?" I say.

"We were there," chirps the ball. (These guys got *zero* bass in their voices. It's kind of hilarious.) "Donny's cousin plays for that team."

"Dummy, don't tell 'em my name!" the bat says.

I snort.

"So you're mad your cuzzo lost?" Laury has come over to join the conversation. "Also, how did you even get here? Midville is like an hour and a half away."

"*We* live around here," the ball says. "So we know all about your little *team*."

"And like I said before," says the bat, "half of you can't even swing. Maybe you'd be decent with a basketball, but don't let that Hank Aaron guy fool you: *this* sport isn't for your people. You only won because those umps felt sorry for you."

This is what I expected in Midville. Wild to find it so much closer to home.

Anyway: it's on now.

"Hey, Quickfire!" I shout over my shoulder. Cala is at first base, but she jogs over.

"Whassup?"

"Seems these *young men* here want to teach *us* how to swing. You up for a few pitches?"

"Of course," she says. And she heads to the mound without another word. I hear the *thunk* of a ball hitting her glove a few moments later.

The short one's eyes widen for a split second, but he recovers quickly. "She barely even caught that," he says. (Lie!)

"So what's the word?" Laury chimes in. "You gonna show us how it's done?"

"Or are you as chicken as that long-butt neck suggests?" from Britt-Marie. Who starts walking around in a circle, poking her head in and out, flapping her elbows behind her, and *bawk-bawk-bawk-BAKAWK*ing.

Didn't think it was possible, but Bat Boy turns even redder.

"I'll show *you* a chicken!" And he storms toward the gate.

Hennessey, who was working catcher, casually hands him a bat as he steps up to the plate, and I jog to take over for her.

What a lot of people don't realize about softball: the relationship between a pitcher and catcher can make or break a game. The pitcher looks at the batter's stance and how they hold the bat from one angle, and the catcher takes note of the batter's swing from a different one. That way they can figure out together—and communicate using agreed-upon hand signals—which pitches are most likely to be strikes.

I pull on my mitt and drop down behind flame-face Lanky McGee.

And I smile.

Not to toot my—our—own horn, but the Quickfire–Lightning pitcher/catcher combo is one of our team's secret weapons.

"You ready, homeboy?" Cala says tauntingly.

"I was born ready," comes his reply.

But he's not.

At all.

Dude doesn't even know how to stand. He sets his feet far too wide, *and* he's crowding the plate.

This is going to be a breeze.

First pitch—a slider—comes so fast, he doesn't even swing all the way through. It's like he panics midway and freezes.

Slight sting of the ball against my palm feels *real* good.

"Strike one!" Coach Nat calls out. She's leaning against the entrance to the dugout with her arms crossed. Clearly waiting for us to get this over with so we can go back to actual practice.

"That's fine," good ol' Donny says, cracking his neck, rolling his shoulders, and shaking out his arms. "I just needed to see what kinda pitching was gonna come at me. Gotta make sure I come with the *right* swing so you'll see how it's really done."

"Uh-huh." I signal for a rising curve. Just to mix things up.

Cala winds and releases, and Skinny Pants (no, for real: this guy's jeans are so snug, you can *see* how long and thin his legs are) swings with all his might.

"Strike two!" from Coach Nat.

"Hey, that was a *ball*!" the round friend cries out. "The pitch was wide to the right!"

"He swung," Laury says.

"Idiot," from Britt.

"Hogan. Cool it," Coach Nat replies . . . but I can hear the smile in her voice.

I throw the ball back to Quickfire and give the same signal as before: rising curve. Might as well give the guy a fighting chance on this third pitch. Now that I see how unwieldy and overpowered *his* swing is, I have zero doubt he'll mistime it and swing too soon.

I'm right.

"Strike THREE, and he's OUTTA THERE!" This time from Britt-Marie.

And just as I expect, he reacts by throwing the bat down and storming off.

"You know what your problem is?" I call out behind him. "You swing like a *boy*—all force and no finesse."

"Yeah, sucka!" Laury shouts.

When I turn to face my team, everyone is high-fiving, and Coach Nat is returning to the mound like nothing happened.

We finish practice with no incident and are all in high spirits during pickup.

But I'd be lying if I said the human bat's comments didn't get under my skin. Especially the one about this sport not being for my "people."

12

Run Batted In

Almost in *spite* of their terrible mascot name, our section semifinal opponents—the Castleberry Crabs—are good.

Like . . . *really* good.

At the top of the fifth inning, we're down three runs. Which isn't *insurmountable*, aka "impossible to overcome," a vocab word we learned in Mr. Bonner's class this week.

But still. My nerves are all jangled.

Speaking of Mr. Bonner, he's at this game. Watching us Firebirds get doused with crustacean-filled salt water. "Let's go, y'all! Head in the diamond!" he shouts from the stands as we take our field positions when it's the Crabs' turn at bat.

It's not that my favorite teacher's *general* presence is distracting for *me*. Might be a different story for Britt-Marie since he's her crush (blegh), and for Laury and Cala since he's their basketball coach, but I've had him for language arts two years in a row, and he's come to games before.

The issue today is that seeing and hearing him reminds me of a conversation he and I had two days ago. A conversation I'd really like to wipe from my memory.

I was leaving the classroom when he called me up to his desk. "Just wanted to check in about the truth you were seeking not too long ago. You make any progress?"

"Oh." And my gaze fell to my favorite pair of well-worn Air Max 90s. "Sort of?" (Completely forgot I'd pretended the "truth-seeker" was someone other than me.)

"You're disappointed?" he asked.

"I mean . . . no?" And I don't know what came over me, but the next thing I knew, stuff was just spilling out. "But also maybe yes? I got more information from the person who sort of set me on this 'truth-seeking' journey in the first place, but I'm not sure what to *do* with it. The really interesting thing is that I might actually have *another* primary source literally under my pillow. Handwritten things are primary sources, right? You taught us that. But I can't bring myself to open the thing because it feels like a super-rude invasion of privacy. I certainly wouldn't want anybody reading *my* journal . . . if it even *is* a journal—"

"Sloooow it down, lovebug." He lifted a hand and stopped me. "Give yourself a second to catch your breath."

"But that's the thing! I don't feel like I *have* a second, Mr. Bonner! I can't stop thinking about it. The story-teller gave me an *assignment*, and deep down, I feel like I'm supposed to complete it, but I have no idea *how*. Or even *why*."

"Fair enough," he said.

"I just know it's become a huge distraction when I'm supposed to be captaining a team—an all-Black one at that—to a league championship title, but now all these differences between Black and white people and the way they've been treated are staring me in the face. I could sort of brush it under the rug before . . . chalk it up to like . . . life 'not being fair.' But it makes me so *angry* now."

"As it should," he replied. "And racism is something you'll definitely have to wrestle with. But you gotta take things a single step at a time."

I took a deep breath.

"Now, I obviously don't know the details regarding this assignment you mention, but I'm a firm believer that if it really is *yours* to complete, the tools and resources you need are either already at your disposal or right within your reach. You just gotta open your eyes and mind a little wider."

That night, I tried to take his advice. I returned to the newspaper clipping and *my* journal, where I'd written as much as I could of what Uncle Jack told me.

But the next thing I knew, I was writing down page after page of my own experiences. Especially the icky-feeling ones that seemed to have something to do with my skin color.

Which brings me back to this game.

The three outs come quick—which is great for us because the deficit we need to overcome doesn't increase. First girl up to bat gets struck out: she hits Cala's fastball, but it's a foul, and the two Quickfire change-ups that come at her back to back are both swings and misses. Second batter pops a gorgeous fly ball, but Noelle manages to snatch it out of the air in deep right field. And then the third Crab manages a sharp grounder, but shortstop Khyler scoops it up and fires it to Laury at first base before homegirl can get there.

Cakewalk.

But once we've changed sides and their pitcher is on the mound, she and I make eye contact as our first batter heads for home plate and takes her stance.

The pitcher is a Black girl. The *only* Black girl on the Castleberry Crab roster.

Her name is Tanisha. Which I only know because I heard someone call it, and I thought they were mispronouncing *my* name, so I turned. It used to happen a *lot* pre-Firebirds, when I was often in her shoes: the only Black girl on *my* team.

I got "SHAY-neese," "Shuh-NICE" (like rhymes with *spice*), "SHAN-niss" . . .

As I watch her windup, the questions I typically try to shove down rise right on up. Do people mispronounce *her* name? Or say things like "Wow, you're great at softball for a girl like you"? Do they touch her hair without permission or make comments about her edges when she sweats and they get frizzy?

What all does Tanisha have to deal with?

"Strike two!" the ump shouts. Our batter (and left-field woman) Clementine takes a second to shake out her shoulders.

I lock my gaze on Tanisha again. Her face is so blank, it's impossible to read. And she's a fantastic pitcher. Definitely well trained and super focused.

But does she feel like an outsider on her team the way I did? The way Great-Grampy JonJon must have at that life-shattering plantation house supper?

We end up winning the game by a single run, all thanks to heavy-hitting Hennessey, who bats Laury in but gets tagged out trying to make her single into a double. (Real go-getter, that one.)

Which means we're going to the 12U section finals.

I can hardly wrap my head around it. And if the quiet buzz in the dugout as we pack up and get ready to head back to the Firebus is any indication, nobody else can, either.

Including Coach Nat. "Ladies, this is . . . this is *huge*," she says as she closes the cooler. "Literal history in the making."

"I mean, we all know Black girls are magic," Britt-Marie chimes in with a shrug. "So it was bound to happen at some point, right?"

"Couldn't have said it better myself." Ms. Erica gives her a side hug.

It's official: an all-Black team has made it to a Dixie Youth Softball Association section championship. If we win, we go to State, and if we win State, we'll represent Georgia in the eight-state league tournament. It would be another first.

As exciting as it all is, it also feels sort of . . . unreal. Like how is it possible to *still* be making this sort of history?

Of course it makes me think of Great-Grampy Jon-Jon and his Major League ambitions. He wouldn't have been the *first* Black man in the MLB—according to my research, there were even a couple prior to Jackie

Robinson. But I wonder if he could *feel* the fact that even receiving that fateful invitation was making history.

When we exit the field, Daddy is standing near the Firebus. Which isn't normal. Parents usually leave right after the game since it's tradition for the team to travel in the Firebus, and our rides need to be at our practice field to take us home when we return there.

Once he spots me, he waves with the hand holding his cane, and then begins to head in our direction.

"Umm . . . Shenice?" Britt-Marie says from beside me.

"Yeah, I dunno, either," I reply.

Ms. Erica walks ahead to meet Daddy halfway and give him a quick hug, and then they talk for a few seconds before she nods and calls me over. "Lightning, baby, come here."

My legs turn to lead, and I'm pretty sure my stomach has relocated itself somewhere inside my cleats.

"You're gonna go with your dad, sweet pea," Ms. Erica says when I reach the two of them. "Fantastic job today, and we'll see you at practice on Monday. Get some rest tomorrow, yeah?" And she rubs my upper arms with both hands.

"But we always ride back from games as a team," I blurt. "Especially when we win."

"And that's not changin', sweet pea," she continues.

"We're just on a bit of a time crunch today, Miss Ma'am. This won't be a regular thing," Daddy says.

I take a deep breath and follow him to his Cadillac. Which currently looks like a low-riding chariot of doom.

"Sorry to take you from your team, baby girl," he says the moment we're inside with the doors shut. "Congratulations, by the way!" He cranks the car. "Headed to the section finals! I'm proud of you, Lightning Lockwood."

I don't respond.

We pull to a stop at the traffic light, and the air changes. I'm not gonna like the reason I'm in this car with him. Or what he has to say. I just know it.

"Daddy, where are we going?" I ask.

He sighs. "Hate to put a damper on your triumph, Shenice," he says. "But I had to take you with *me* because our uncle Jack . . ."

Oh no.

"Well, we learned today that he's dying."

13

Playbook

The brown leather book *is* a journal. And it did belong to Great-Grampy JonJon.

I know that now because I read every single entry inside it when we return home from the hospital.

Uncle Jack, as it turns out, has kidney disease. Which Mama and Daddy both knew but didn't tell me.

Not sure how I feel about that yet.

He was asleep when Daddy and I got to the room he's sharing with another elderly man, and he stayed that way the whole time we were there. But the tube attached to his arm, and a different one wrapped around his ears with prongs stuck up his nose, and the hanging bag of clear liquid drip-drip-dripping beside his bed? Seeing that stuff made me feel itchy all over.

I stood there watching Uncle Jack, while Daddy talked with the doctor. It was my first time really getting to look at his face from the front; I usually only see the left side when he's talking to me because I sit on his couch while he's in a chair, facing forward.

He's been alive a long time, Uncle Jack has. I could see it in the deep grooves in his skin. The little bit of hair he has is white as cotton and of a similar texture. And as I stared at his shut eyelids, I thought about all the terrible things he probably saw as a person who not only watched his big brother's life get ripped apart, but lived through stuff like the Civil Rights Movement we learned about in social studies. He was even around when it was illegal for Black people to use the same water fountains as white people. Or eat in certain restaurants. Or, as he mentioned in his story, sit in the same section of the bus.

I know he and I only talked a couple of times, but as I stood there, I started to cry. I wouldn't have been able to put into words *why*, but it felt like a new weight had settled on my shoulders. Jack watched JonJon's dreams crumble and couldn't do anything about it, even with *proof* of his big bro's innocence.

He and my great-grandpa had to face such horrible stuff, even though they hadn't done anything *wrong.*

The whole thing made me so mad, I felt like smoke might shoot from my ears, and if I parted my lips even the slightest bit, fire would roar up from my stomach and burn the whole place down.

Daddy came back into the room while I was fuming. "He's still out, huh?" he said. And then he sighed. "We'll come back tomorrow."

By the time we reached the car, I was ready to explode.

"Why didn't y'all tell me he was sick?" I said the second we were buckled in.

At this, Daddy turned to me. Looked me right in the eye and said, "Shenice, we weren't sure how to."

"Yeah, well, that's not a good excuse." I crossed my arms and faced the window as more tears ran down my cheeks. And in *that* moment, I knew I was crying because I didn't know what I was supposed to do.

Daddy was quiet for a few seconds. When he spoke again, it was in a voice so low, I knew it was important that I listen. He said, "It was a harder call to make than you think, baby girl. You're a brilliant kid with a lot going on. Yes, your mother could've mentioned that Jack was sick before you met him the first time, but . . . well, we wanted you to pay attention to him. I know you'll wanna dispute what I'm about to say, but me and your mama have both *been* twelve, Shenice. If you'd known he was sick, there was a chance you would've written the old man off."

"But, Daddy—"

"I know. What we hoped would happen did: you liked being around him and asked if you could go back. Which I know means you're attached now. And all of this hurts."

I *really* got to crying then.

"But, baby, the truth is Jack's been here for so long, we weren't expecting this, either."

I was permitted to go straight to my room and shut my door when we got home, and before I could think about it too much, I pulled the brown book from beneath my pillow and began to read.

JonJon hadn't written very frequently at first: it seems he started shortly after returning from his military service, but there are weeks—and sometimes months—between the first handful of entries.

He talks about being treated poorly overseas, despite the fact that he enlisted to prove he cared about his country. And he also mentioned feeling like he was treated even worse once he returned home.

Things turn lighter when he starts writing about getting back into baseball, and my favorite entries are the ones where he talks about meeting my great-grandmother, Betsy, and the one after she tells him she's *"with child."*

"I'm just as giddy as a gumdrop!" he says after that one. And it makes me smile: now I know where Daddy got the phrase from.

Up until the Carlyle thing, the entries aren't too terrible. There's a line in one—*"Seems white folks can't believe I had the audacity to hope the laying of my life on the line would actually mean something"*—that gets my blood boiling, but overall, it's clear he was just recording bits of his life.

What I find myself reading over and over again, though, are five entries *interspersed* (gotta love those Bonner vocab words) with a bunch of other ones. The first is about when Jackie Robinson went to the MLB and the world of possibility it opened, but as they progress, Great-Grampy JonJon details occurrences that match Uncle Jack's story.

The last entry in the group makes my chest hurt. It's seems to be written right after JonJon is basically blotted out of the Negro Leagues. And while he held on to his trophies, pictures, and trunk full of equipment and paraphernalia, he mentions wanting to "just forget about everything."

He wrote a few times after that: mostly about things like money troubles, exhaustion, and how hard it was to be a family man. But it's clear that the light inside him had gone out.

It's the saddest I've ever felt.

Knowing my PopPop—who I'm guessing was the kid in Great-Grandma Betsy's belly—went on to play baseball and that Daddy followed in *his* footsteps makes me feel a tiny bit better. That lying Jacob Carlyle might've hit pause on Great-Grampy JonJon's dreams, but they lived on in his son and grandson.

They live on in me.

By the time I've read the last page, I've made a decision.

And while it may not bring about any justice or clear the name of Jumpin' JonJon Lockwood, Uncle Jack is still here. The least I can do is find that dumb DiMaggio glove so that when Jack does pass on, *he'll* be able to rest in peace.

Uncle Jack's awake when we get there the next afternoon. And at first, I'm excited: I really only need one piece of information from him.

Sadly, when we step into his room and he looks in our direction, I can tell he's not really here today.

There's a doctor beside his bed, checking his blood pressure and stuff, and as we enter, she turns to us and smiles. "I'm guessing you're the grandnephew Mr. Lock-wood's been bragging on? Victor?"

My ears perk up.

Apparently, so do Daddy's. "He was talking about me?" he says. And I turn to look at him because I've never heard him sound this way before. Like a kid learning his favorite superhero is not only real, but knows his name.

It makes me feel strange inside, knowing my big, strong daddy sees someone else the way I see him.

"He talked about you all morning," the doctor says. Then her gaze shifts to me, and I swear my heart stops beating. "You too," she says. "You're Victor's daughter, yeah? And you're some sort of ballplayer?"

I can't help it: a smile splits my face without my permission. "Yeah," I say. "Softball."

"Oh, yeah? What position?"

"I'm a catcher."

"Well, that sure is awesome." Now *she's* beaming. "I have a softball player at home. Shortstop. I don't make it to many games because I spend so much time here, but her travel team had a pretty solid record this year. The Stockwood Sharks," she says with pride, but maybe also a little bit of mockery. And who could blame her. It is an interesti—

Wait.

"Stockwood Sharks, you say?"

She reads the monitor thing next to Uncle Jack's bed. "I know. Team name's a little tacky."

No. Way.

And she said shortstop . . . "Does your daughter have really shiny golden hair?"

"Put like that, she sounds like a unicorn." The doctor laughs. "But yes, she does."

Britt is never going to believe this.

"Why do you ask?" the doctor says.

I don't want to reveal that my team lost to her daughter's not too long ago, so I make something up. "Oh, umm . . . I can just see that yours is blond, so I wondered if your daughter's maybe was, too. I certainly look like *my* mom."

"Ah." She grabs her clipboard and heads for the door. "Well, we're gonna hope for *my* daughter's sake that she ages more gracefully. Mr. Lockwood, a word if you would, please."

They step out of the room, and the door shuts behind them.

So I take my chance. "Uncle Jack?" I say, moving a single shaky step closer to the bed.

He turns his head toward the sound, but I'm 98 percent sure he doesn't really see me. Makes my heart sink like that big ship that hit an iceberg underwater.

"Shenice?" The sound comes from behind me.

Daddy.

"We gotta run, baby girl. Uncle Jack is being moved back to his apartment at the assisted-living facility and put in hospice. We need to make sure there are groceries and things of that nature."

Hospice. No idea what that is, but it doesn't sound good. I sigh and take one last look at the old man before going to meet Daddy at the door.

The doctor is still at the nurse's station when we pass. "We appreciate your help, Doc," Daddy says.

"Don't even mention it, Mr. Lockwood," she replies. "And I'll do as you requested and put a memo in his file for all medical personnel to take note of his lucid stretches over the next twenty-four hours."

"Can't thank you enough," Daddy replies.

"It's truly my pleasure," the doctor says.

And that's it. We walk away from the nurse's station and toward the exit like *the last living Lockwood man in his generation* isn't all alone behind us.

"Oh, Mr. Lockwood! I almost forgot. . . ." The doctor breaks into a light jog and reaches us in no time. "The elder Mr. Lockwood wrote something down earlier and asked me to give it to Shenice."

"That's me!" I reply, stepping forward, maybe a smidge too excited.

She smiles. "That's what I thought, Lightning." She winks and hands me a folded piece of paper that looks like it was torn from the edge of a legal pad. "Congrats on that section final, by the way." And she strides off.

Before I can process that my great-granduncle's doctor has a daughter who plays for one of only three teams who beat us in the regular season—and that Dr. Mom likely knew it all along—I've opened the thing up.

Once I see what's on it, I have to force myself to keep my feet moving so I don't collapse in the middle of the hospital corridor.

Daddy would ask questions.

And I can't have him asking questions. Not right now.

Because what's on that scrap of paper

. . . is an address.

14

Stealing Home

The interesting thing about living in a city that's always changing: the shiny new stuff makes it easy to miss small things that stay the same.

Example: our home field is in a new park near Coach Nat's school. It opened two seasons ago. The same year we started as a team.

That park is a quarter-mile from the massive, futuristic-looking stadium that's home to our city's NFL and MLS teams. There are big new houses springing up all around this area, but since we live in a different part of town, I'm not here enough to really notice the changes as they happen.

Or *aren't* happening.

Case in point: the house appears to be a mere five-minute walk from where I pour my Lockwood heart and soul out on the practice diamond four days per week.

It wasn't easy to find. For one, the street name has changed. The note from Uncle Jack says Ashby Place, but now it's named for somebody "Burruss Sr." This is definitely a *thing* in my city: honoring somebody by renaming a street after them.

I only know it's the right street because I told Daddy I'm working on an Atlanta history project, and there was supposedly some major historical event during the Civil Rights Movement that happened "on a street called Ashby Place, but I can't find it on Google Maps."

He drew back a bit. "Really now?"

Knew I was treading on dangerous ground, but I shrugged and said, "That's what the internet said."

"And what does the internet say happened on Ashby Place?"

Definitely hadn't anticipated *that* question (which, thinking about it now, was pretty dumb). So I just threw something out there: "A leader's house was firebombed. At least according to what I read."

"Huh," he replied. "Well, I'll tell *you* something that old internet doesn't know: your PopPop grew up on Ashby Place."

"Wait, really?" (The surprise was genuine. I figured the address was to the house Uncle Jack mentioned, but I didn't expect PopPop to be connected to it.)

"Sure did. Your Great-Grampy JonJon and Uncle Jack grew up there as well, believe it or not. When his mother died, JonJon moved back to that house and raised *my* daddy in it."

"Have you ever been there?" I asked before I could think better of it.

"Once," he said. "When I was about twelve."

"Does another family live in it now?"

"Oh noooo. Far as I know, our family still owns the place. In fact . . ." His eyebrows pulled together. "I wonder if the deed is in Uncle Jack's name. Guess I better find out."

And before he could run off in pursuit of this particular bit of grown-up stuff, I said, "So, wait, where's the street?"

"Oh, it's called T P Burruss Senior Drive Southwest now," he said. "And I wanna see this project when you finish. I had no idea a civil rights leader lived on the same street where my daddy grew up. Seems like the sort of thing he woulda mentioned . . ."

Uh-oh.

"Maybe he had a good reason not to?" I said. "Especially if the house was set on fire. Maybe it was too bad a memory to bring up?"

"Maybe . . . ," Daddy said absentmindedly. But he did leave the room.

Thankfully, the house number hadn't changed: once I had the updated street name, it popped right up. Zero-point-two miles from the place I needed to be at four o'clock the following afternoon.

At first, things go a bit *too* smoothly. Daddy's preoccupied with Uncle Jack stuff, so he doesn't question why I have him drop me off thirty minutes early. And the address truly is only a five-minute walk away, just like the map app says it is.

But the "house" I find at said address is . . . well, it's clear no one lives here.

In fact, if the wooden and graffitied boards over the windows and doors are any indication, nobody's lived here for a long time.

No one's lived in any of these houses.

The one to the right is also boarded up. It's got greenery around the sides and back and looks like it's being reclaimed by nature.

The one next door on the left is only halfway there. While I made up that whole firebomb story, there was *definitely* an actual fire inside of it.

The house across the street has a half-sunken roof covered in a blue plastic thing. The one on *its* left is being devoured by ivy, and the one to the right . . . no longer exists.

In fact, Jack and JonJon's—and PopPop's—childhood home is the most *together* house on this street. The not-so-great news: the sagging porch and drooping roof make it pretty clear that just waltzing in and finding the right room isn't the smartest idea.

A lump forms in my throat, and I have to shut my eyes to keep from crying.

Uncle Jack is dying. Half the time when he's awake, he's not making a ton of sense. It's not that I don't believe Great-Grampy JonJon's career was ruined by a missing Joe DiMaggio glove that he didn't steal. There's enough "primary source" evidence—the newspaper and journal—to piece all that together.

But this whole thing about Jack retrieving the glove and not telling anybody, then hiding it beneath a floorboard in his and JonJon's shared childhood bedroom?

The longer I stand here, staring up at this crumbling place, the more this whole thing seems way out of left field.

And yet I can't seem to just . . . walk away. Because what if Uncle Jack is telling the truth? What if he's spent his whole life with this *thing* draped over his back like some grungy coat of lead . . . and *I* could take it off for him by being the person who *listened* and *believed*?

On the day we cast votes for team captain, Coach Nat made us write down the reason behind our picks. When I was chosen—almost unanimously (I voted for

Cala, and Hennessey and Khyler had made an agreement to vote for each other)—Coach had everyone tell me their reasons for choosing me. And though it was super uncomfortable hearing my teammates say nice things about me, most of their reasons were similar. Laury summed it up best: "Lightning's a good listener, and she believes in us."

I want to spin on my Air Maxes and haul my butt back to my regular life—back to the practice field and my epic teammates and a state championship to win.

But I can't.

Because I believe in Uncle Jack. He wanted to help his brother, but he couldn't. Not back then.

Now he just wants someone to know—and believe—that he tried.

Maybe that's why this place is tugging at me. To the point that I've somehow moved from the sidewalk near the street, up the cracked walkway, to the base of the porch steps. I don't try to climb them, because who's to say they won't break apart beneath my feet and drop me down into some abyss where I'll have to slay giant underground rodents with my bat.

(Hard pass on *that*, thanks.)

I *do* step into the knee-high grass—if you can even call the crunchy brown stuff grass—and head around the right side of the house.

There are three windows here, all sealed up tight

with pieces of wood: two at waist level that I assume lead to different rooms, and one near the ground that I guess goes to some kind of crawl space like the one at our house. The ground doesn't slope down enough for it to be a basement.

I continue around to the backyard. There's a rear door at ground level with a window on each side of it. Both windows are tightly sealed.

But the door . . .

I take a step closer.

There *is* a large wooden plank over the door, but it's not sealed. At all.

In fact, as I get closer, I see that the plank itself is cracked. Pretty sure if I pulled at the edge, it would swing open like a door.

I take a couple more steps. Then I use the toe of my shoe to pull at the corner of the plank. It moves toward me.

One more step.

I lean to the right to peek behind the plank.

The back door is framed in blue wood, but the center of it is frosted glass.

Said glass is broken and sticking out in jagged shards, but I can see straight inside to the darkness beyond.

I reach for my cell phone in my back pocket, intending to use the little flashlight.

But then comes the low rumble of a growl.

And now I can't breathe.

Slowly, carefully, I turn my head to peek over my shoulder. Behind me is the biggest, scariest dog I've ever seen. A rottweiler. Which I only know because Hennessey has one that does nothing but eat, poop, and sleep.

This one is doing none of the above . . . but the bared teeth *do* make me think it might be hungry.

"Uhhh . . ." I slowly rotate my body so I'm facing the dog. "Okay, boy—"

It growls louder.

"Girl? Are you a girl?" Hands up in surrender. "My bad. Listen, I'm just gonna go now, cool? No harm, no foul . . ."

I start to lower my arms, but the dog tenses up. And barks.

"Okay, okay, okay! Your house! I get it, I swear!" I say. "You stay right there, and I'll get out of your fur."

I step left, and my foot lands on something hard. Which makes me wobble.

The dog lunges, and every move that follows slips into slow motion: I'm falling. My right shoulder hits something that causes a *snap*, and then there's a searing pain in my left forearm.

The world goes white, and I shut my eyes.

I know I'm on my back, and there's a heavy weight on my chest. I can hear the sound of barking. But it's far off.

And fading.

Soon I can't hear anything at all.

15

Safe

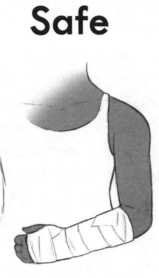

When I *can* hear again, it starts with the sound of a steady *beep . . . beep . . . beep . . .*

Then come the voices.

"Oh my gosh, I think her hand moved!"

"Wait, for real?"

"*Yes!* Look at her eyes!"

"Oh, snap, she's right! They're moving around under there. . . ."

That's a boy's voice. And it ain't squeaky-sounding like Drake's.

I force my eyelids open. And I really do mean *force:*

it's more difficult than I think it's ever been. Like they're cemented shut or something.

"Look, look, look, she's waking up!"

"Thank goodness!"

The first thing I see is a ceiling like the ones in school: plaster tile rectangles spotted with holes and separated by thin metal strips. The beep draws my eyes to a monitor screen with lit green numbers and a jagged line that spikes with each *boop!* Above that is a plastic sack full of clear liquid with a tube hanging from the bottom.

A tube that hangs down and leads . . . into the crook of my elbow.

The beeping gets faster.

"Sheesh, Lockwood." There's a swat on my left shoulder. It sends a shooting pain down into my palm.

"Owwww," I groan. I also groan on the inside: my voice sounds like I've been breathing chalk dust.

"Oh my god, girl! I'm so sorry!"

"Yo, Britt, can you mellow out? Sorry about her, Lightning. You know she been worried half to death."

Once my vision clears from the pain, I see two girls standing on the left side of the railed bed I'm in. One with light brown skin, perfect sandy blond ringlet curls, and green eyes, and the other deep brown with braids in a backward ball cap.

Britt-Marie and Laury.

"Okay, look here," Britt-Marie says, crossing her arms the moment we meet eyes. "Like . . . my bad for hitting your hurt arm or whatever. But you've been acting the *epitome* of shady lately, and nobody's said anything because Ms. Erica told us you have a sick uncle or something. But this is *too far*, and I swear, if you ever scare us like that again—"

"Not the time, Britt! Dang!" This from Laury. She shoves Britt-Marie.

I would laugh if it didn't hurt so much to move.

"How are you feeling, Shenice?"

My head whips right faster than I thought it could.

It's Scoob. Standing on the other side of what is clearly my hospital bed.

Why am I in the hospital?

"Your dad found you passed out behind an abandoned house near your practice park," Scoob says. (Did I ask that question out loud?) "You had a nasty gash in your arm, and a giant dog at your side—like she was watching over you, your dad said. I think you might have a new pet, actually."

"My *dad* found me?"

"He sure did," Laury says.

"When *somebody* didn't show up to practice, Coach Nat got worried," says Britt-Marie.

"We all did." Laury again. "So she called your pops.

Who said he dropped you off and watched you walk onto the field."

"And of course we *all* started freaking *all* the way out because you'd *clearly* been kidnapped. Like what else could've happened?" from Britt-Marie.

Laury rolls her eyes. "Within three minutes, your pops called back and told us not to panic because he was pretty sure he knew where you were—"

"So then we waited like *fifteen minutes* for him to call back *again*—"

"And when he did, he said he'd found you. And he was taking you to the hospital."

What on earth *happened*?

"Practice was canceled, obviously," Britt-Marie says with a dismissive wave. "Laur and I caught a ride here with Coach Nat and Ms. Erica. Like, what were you even doing, Shenice? You could've *died*!"

"Britt-Marieeeee . . . ," from Laury.

I turn to Scoob. How did *he* get here? How did he even know *I* was here? I want to ask but can't get the words to form.

"I was gaming online with Drake," he says (again reading my mind?), "and he suddenly goes, 'Oh, crap, something happened to my sister.' It's the first time I've ever used your mom's cell number. She picked me up on the way here." He looks me right in the eye now. "This about that thing we talked about?"

"What *thing*? Why don't I know about a *thing*?" Britt-Marie's cheeks have gone all rosy.

"Real smooth, Scoob-a-doob," I say.

"Sorry!"

"Still waiting to hear about this *thing* William knows that I don't." Britt-Marie crosses her arms.

"Y'all gotta relaaaaaax," Laury says. "Our captain is injured and needs her rest!"

I look down at my left arm. It's bandaged from around my thumb to just shy of my elbow.

And now I can't breathe. The beeping sound speeds up.

Our first state tournament game is in a week.

"Oh no, oh no, oh no," I say.

Britt-Marie waves my panic off. "Your arm is fine. You just got eleven stitches."

"Eleven stitches?!"

"Eleven stitches," Laury confirms.

"The cut in your arm wasn't super long, but it was pretty deep," Scoob replies. "And you hit your head when you passed out, but I heard the doctor say no concussion. You lost a good bit of blood and needed fluids, though." He points at the bag of liquid slowly dripping into the tube in my arm. "Gotta drink more water."

Has he always had that cute mole under his eye? is what goes through my head, though I don't say it. Hopefully he doesn't read *that* thought.

"Well, now that we have established what Shenice Ashley Lockwood is doing *here*," Britt says, "perhaps we can move on to why you were at that creepy house?"

This girl is so relentless.

"And talk fast. No telling when they're gonna kick us out." She looks at the door. "Your dad had to pull some 'old baseball buddy' strings with the doctor—who is apparently his college teammate—to get permission for us to be in here in the first place. Won't surprise me at all if they suddenly snatch it away—"

And at the sound of those three words—"snatch it away"—everything crashes over me. Great-Grampy Jon-Jon's opportunity being snatched away, and Uncle Jack having to sit back and watch. PopPop having to end his career before he wanted to, and Daddy's chances at the MLB being snatched away by that injury.

And then there's me: team captain whose attempt at *saving the day* has landed me with a stitched-up catching arm a week before my team's first state tournament game.

Did I just *snatch away* our chance at the league championship?

I look at my bandage again and burst into tears.

"Whoa, whoa! It's gonna be okay, Lightning!" Laury says. "We promise!"

"Yeah, don't cry, babe!"

"Oh, now you're telling her not to cry after poppin' off on her, Britt?" (Oh, Laury.)

"Ladies, ladies, ladies," from Scoob. "I can respect that you're different people with different approaches to communication. But our friend is in distress here. Perhaps you can set aside your differences for a few so we can figure out how to be helpful?"

Britt-Marie and Laury both draw back in surprise, then look at each other before shifting their gazes between me and him and starting to smirk and make their eyebrows dance.

"*William* does have a point," Britt-Marie says to me with an obnoxious and obvious wink. "So . . . how do we help?"

I look around at my three closest friends, and my eyes well with tears again. Happy ones this time. "Okay," I say.

And I tell them everything.

16

Windup

Six days.

That's how long we have before our first state matchup.

What I *don't* know, though, is how much longer we have with Uncle Jack.

As it turns out, part of the reason I woke up to my friends instead of my parents in my hospital room is because Uncle Jack was in the process of being discharged. When Daddy came back to get me, he told me Uncle Jack was on his way to his apartment. That he'd be there, in that *hospice* thing—which I learned is special care for people who aren't expected to live much longer—until he . . . isn't anymore.

"Could be weeks, or could be days," Daddy said. "Impossible to say, really."

It's been three days since *I* woke up in the hospital with my left hand and forearm looking like I'd shoved it in a cloud, and despite my *throwing* arm—and catching *hand*—being perfectly fine, I'm not allowed to do anything at practices but "stay seated" (Mama's words).

Watch the magic happen without me.

From the dugout. Because apparently, anywhere outside of it puts me "at unnecessary risk." (You'd swear I'd broken all my bones, the way the grown-ups are acting.)

So I sit. And I strategize.

A few things have fallen into place—things that I hope are more *divine intervention* than *some ancient family curse leading me into a trap that's gonna end my batball career.* First, two days ago, as Britt-Marie and I sat in the dugout, trying to figure out how to get in the house without going *in* the house, Khyler—who'd been standing right in front of us totally unnoticed—cleared her throat, and said: "Not that I was *listening*, but Hen and I have a robot prototype that could go into a place but be controlled from outside."

Epic.

Second, just last night, I found something useful in Great-Grampy JonJon's trunk.

In truth, I don't even know what I was searching for. Daddy was gone, and Mama was working in her office, so I decided to take a chance, figuring that if I got caught, I could make up something about wanting to see PopPop's room again so I could understand him more. Though Mama and Daddy have yet to really ask me any questions about why I went to *that* house (clearly it is *not* the one I said was firebombed during the Civil Rights Movement), I don't think they'd bat an eye at my room-trespassing excuse. Grown-ups love that mushy stuff.

I didn't even look around once I got inside. Just made a beeline for the door to the attic space. And once I was up there, I zeroed in on the chest.

There was way more interesting stuff in there than one would expect. A pair of plastic red binoculars with a lens missing, an old Scrabble set, and a Magic 8 Ball. (Me: *"Is this whole glove hunt thing stupid?"* Ball: *"Better not tell you now."* So much for predicting the future . . .) There was also a set of marbles, a baseball wrapped in tissue paper with a *lot* of signatures on it, and a box of Cracker Jack so old, I dropped it out of disgust the second I realized what it was.

But none of that stuff compared to what I found when I removed a pile of framed pictures so I could see to the bottom of the trunk. There, inside a plastic sleeve, was a sheet of paper with a drawing of the house where I'd sliced my arm, and a blueprint-style sketch of its lay-out below it.

I knew the place seemed small from the outside, but I didn't realize *how* small: it has two bedrooms and one bathroom, in addition to a small living room and kitchen.

That's it.

Provided there were no renovations, we basically have a map now and know exactly which two rooms to send the robot into. The tricky part will be finding the loose floorboard—if it's still loose—and getting it lifted so we can see underneath it. (I feel silly even saying all this, but my friends being all in is helpful. I think. . . .)

And third: the moment my butt hits the bench in the dugout this afternoon—you know, for this practice I'm sitting out of—Britt-Marie appears in front of me. Arms crossed, her expression just as smug as when she tricked her grandpa into buying her that expensive bat. "We don't have to worry about our quest cover story or transportation," she says.

My face scrunches in confusion. "We don't?"

"Nope. I got us covered." And she looks at her nails.

This oughta be good. . . .

"Do tell," I say, taking the bait. (She's so dramatic.)

"Well, over the past couple of weeks, I've *sworn* there was a skunk who would show up right beneath my cracked bedroom window every time my parents were gone. And last night, I got fed up and decided I would chase it away. Except what I *found* was my idiot stepbro, Sebastian, engaged in an activity his father would find *most* unseemly were he to ever hear about it. So now he owes me a favor for keeping his smelly smoke secret."

"Huh," I say. "Impressive."

"Mm-hmm." And she turns and struts onto the field to take her position.

Which means we have the what (robot), the where (layout), and the how (Sebastian) of #OperationDiMaggio, as Scoob calls it.

Just gotta figure out the *when*.

Cala throws one heck of a heater, and Laury, who is filling in for me at catcher, leaps to her feet and snatches the glove from her hand. "Oww! Bruh, this is *practice*. Take it *easy*!" she shouts.

"Nothing about this is gonna be *easy*," Coach Nat shouts back.

She can certainly say that again.

The day of the mission, things start to go wrong almost immediately.

Hennessey, Khyler, Scoob, and I meet at Britt-Marie's house as planned. (Laury is on cover-story duty in case we wind up late for practice.) But Sebastian initially isn't down with "shlepping five tweeny-boppers across town to only God knows where. There aren't even enough seatbelts."

Britt-Marie quickly nips this in the bud. "Umm, perhaps you think I'm denser than that *grease* you slather on your hair in pursuit of 'sea-sickening waves,' but let us not forget that you had a group of girls five-deep in the backseat—on each other's *laps*—when you picked me up from practice three days ago. If you wanna get technical *now*, I can certainly tell Daddy about *that*, in addition to the *other* thing—"

"All right, all right!" Sebastian scowls something serious but complies with Britt's demands. Even puts the doors on the Jeep so none of us "fall out and become preteen roadkill."

(So kind of him.)

The ride there is a lot . . . with Sebastian asking twenty questions about what we're doing and why we didn't just go after softball practice since "the place is so close"; Scoob sitting in the passenger seat constantly peeking over his shoulder at me; Khyler and Hennessey double-, triple-, and quadruple-checking to make sure the bot is "in working order"; and Britt-Marie holding my hand—which for some reason is making my heart beat faster, just like it does when Scoob looks at me. Not that I have time to think about that right now.

Being twelve is hard.

Once we arrive and get around to the back, we're

faced with a problem I should've seen coming, but didn't.

And it's not the dog. The dog, who *I* had the privilege of renaming Lightning, is ours now. She's currently at the vet getting her shots. (And man, do I hate it for her.)

No, the issue we encounter is this: the broken board over the back door has been replaced with a new, very much *not* broken plank of wood. That is sealed very tightly.

"Well, crap on a cracker," Hennessey says.

"No worries," from Britt-Marie. "Go ahead and set up. We'll have that outta the way in a jiffy." And she bounds off. "BRB!"

"You heard her, Hen," Khyler says, setting her duffel bag on the ground. "Let's get to work." And they do.

Which leaves me sort of alone with Scoob. Who is suddenly close enough for me to feel his arm brush against mine. I swallow. Hard.

"How you been feeling, Neece-Neece?" he says, using the nickname he used to call me when we were in kindergarten. Which sparks all these swirly-tummy *feelings*. "That arm healing up okay?"

"Yeah. It's good." I look down at it. On day two, I switched over from having my entire forearm wrapped in white gauze to what's basically a giant Band-Aid. "Having stitches is weird. My arm already spit one out."

Scoob laughs. "Gross."

"Yeah."

"It's cool what you're doing for your uncle," he says. "I hope you know that. You're a good niece." His voice dips. "I'm sure it means more to him than you know."

I glance over. Scoob's eyes are sad now. He lost his grandma—the one who used to live next door to me— around this time last year.

"I appreciate you saying that," I reply. "I just hope this isn't a wild goose chase, you know?"

"Will you stop acting like I'm trying to *murder* you?" Britt-Marie's voice rings out. "Like, dang!"

"This is *trespassing*, BM. And it's *illegal*." A patronizing male voice.

Is she bringing Sebastian back here?!

"Yeah, well, what you were doing is, too. So suck it up. And stop calling me that."

They appear, Britt-Marie looking triumphant as she leads her stepbrother, who is carrying a pair of black metal rod things—one L-shaped with a flattened end, and a second straight, round one—with an expression on his face that matches Drake's when he's told he doesn't get to *decide* he's not going to the dentist.

I almost laugh at how much control Britt-Marie has right now.

Five minutes and a sweaty Sebastian later, the plank has been pulled aside.

"Whoa," Britt-Marie says.

Because the door I sliced my arm on . . . is gone. Completely.

"Well, at least we know the entry is easy," Khyler says. "You ready, Hen?"

"Yup."

They position the robot, which looks like a super-fancy version of that movie robot WALL-E—it's got a bright orange, boxlike central piece, with arms that end in movable claws, and wheels wrapped in that flat chain stuff you see on bulldozers. A head sticks up out of the top, and it has eyes, *eyelashes*, and pouty red lips painted on. "Everyone, meet Valentina," Hennessey says, setting it down just inside the empty doorway.

Khyler shows us the tablet she'll use to control the thing. "Happy to report that she's fully charged and ready to roll," she says. "And she'll give us eyes in the dark. As you can see, she lights up, and there are six cameras— one on each side, one underneath, and one between her eyes—that combine to give us a three-hundred-sixty-degree view of her surroundings. With night vision."

"This is pretty epic," Scoob says.

And he's not wrong.

Within a few minutes, we've gotten a decent lay of the land. The back door leads into what was the kitchen, though there are no doors on the cabinets, the fridge looks straight out of an episode of the show *Leave It to*

Beaver (Daddy used to make us watch it with him so we could see "how things used to be"), and there's a hole where I'd guess a stove would go.

Valentina trucks into the living room space, which still has sheet-covered shapes of what I'm guessing are a couch, chair, and coffee table. The house is chock-full of dust and debris, but not as run-down on the inside as I expected, considering how old it is. When I was coming into our kitchen yesterday morning, I overheard Daddy talking to Mama about how "*sturdy* that place still seems. They used to build stuff to last."

"Hang a left into that little hallway," I say.

Once Khyler does, we see three open doorways. To the left is the small bathroom; with the light shining on it, we can see that the tub and tiles are all powder blue. To the right of the bathroom is the door to bedroom number one. And right beside it is the door to bedroom number two.

"Any idea which room?" Hennessey says.

"We'll have to check both." I force my voice past the softball-ish lump of fear in my throat.

"K. We'll start with the one on the left, I guess." And Khyler maneuvers Valentina into the bedroom closest to the bathroom. It's pitch-black because the two windows that appear on the layout are boarded up from the outside.

"Does the light get any brighter?" I say.

"Little bit," from Khyler. Who turns it up as bright as it will go.

Lasts just long enough for us to see the desk Valentina is approaching along the back wall before she hits something on the floor and tips onto her side.

The light shuts off.

"Aww, man. Aww, man," Hennessey says. "No, no, no."

The tablet screen goes black.

And there goes our robot.

17

Bottom of the Sixth

Practice over the next few days is nothing short of *abysmal* (definitely got *that* one right on this week's vocab test). It's *so* bad that halfway through day two of poor throws, missed catches, and "single-butt-cheek effort," as Coach Nat puts it, she makes everyone toss their equipment on the pitcher's mound and run laps around the field.

Myself included.

"I don't know what's going on with you Firebirds," she shouts as we run, "but last I checked, *you* told *me* that *you* want to take this team to the DYSA championship. I'm gonna hold you to your *WORD*."

"Bruh, she might be bout to kill us with all this running," Laury pants behind me.

"Just keep going," from Cala. Who's actually *on* her game today. Homegirl has been throwing straight *heat*.

Can't say the same for Khyler, who's subbing at catcher. It's been pretty tragic to watch. The number of times the ball has zipped past her and *clanged* against the back fence is . . . well, that's certainly part of the reason we're running laps.

Coach shouts again. "We've only got two practices left after today! Do y'all *want* this, or do you *WANT* it?" she says.

Thing is, after the robot fiasco at the old house, all this softball stuff just . . . doesn't feel like it matters as much. Not that I could say so out loud to anyone, but something about getting *so close* to (potentially) finding what Uncle Jack asked me to look for made me realize that I *do* care about clearing my great-grandpa's name.

Even if no one but Uncle Jack really knows it.

Daddy's pretty clueless. I worked up the nerve to ask him if he knew why Great-Grampy JonJon stopped playing baseball, and his face scrunched up as though he'd never thought about it before. "Well, I'm guessing it was the same reason *my* daddy stopped playing. Ballplayers back then—especially Black ones—didn't earn what the pros do now, and my presumption is that old JonJon couldn't make a real living."

To be honest, my first reaction to this was: *What if this is a wild goose chase?* I struggled to believe *no one*—not Great-Grampy JonJon, Uncle Jack, or PopPop—ever told Daddy JonJon's story.

But then last night, the strangest thing happened: Scoob called to check on me. And just like before, on the porch, everything I was thinking and feeling spilled out.

Which is when Scoob told me some things about his grandma—*may her soul rest in peace*, as the grown-ups say—that I never would've expected. And he swore me to secrecy, because it's stuff not even Scoob's dad (aka his grandma's son) is aware of. "In *my* experience, sometimes grown-ups don't tell kids certain things because they know it's gonna change how we see them," Scoob said. "And I'm not saying I *agree* with that, but after learning what I did about my G'ma, I understood why she never told my dad."

My case is different, obviously: Great-Grampy Jon-Jon didn't actually do anything wrong. But Scoob still had a point: maybe he didn't tell my PopPop or Daddy because he didn't want to discourage them or something. Or maybe it was just too painful.

And maybe the same was true for Uncle Jack . . . or maybe JonJon *asked* Jack not to tell anyone. Scoob helped me see another side of *this*, too: "Perhaps he realized he wasn't gonna be around a lot longer the same way my G'ma did. So he needed to get the whole story—and his part in it—off his chest—"

"And he saw *me* as the person who could do something about it," I said.

"Right."

(Sidenote: I wish Scoob *would* propose like that eighth grader did to Britt-Marie.)

Anyway, with all that on my mind, is it any wonder I can't focus on a game I might not even be allowed to play?

And Hennessey and Khyler lost the robotics project they've been working on for over a year. When Valentina took her topple, Hennessey jumped up, determined to waltz right into the house and rescue the bot, but Sebastian stopped her. Said he "refused to be held responsible for a little kid getting injured in an abandoned death trap."

I have no idea what Hennessey and Khyler told their parents, if anything at all, but I think it's safe to say the loss is hitting Hen the hardest: midway through yesterday's practice—the first half of which she spent staring off into space and missing easy catches—she complained of a stomachache and asked to sit the rest out.

Today, she didn't even bother to take the field.

"Hey, Shenice?" Britt-Marie pants as she runs up

beside me on our third lap. "I don't think Hennessey's okay."

"Yeah, me either," I say.

"Is there anything we can do?"

As we round into left field, I have a straight-on view of the park's entrance. Hang a left onto the main road, walk up a block and turn right, and the old house is the fifth lot up on the right.

So close . . . and yet so far away.

"No, Britt," I say, fighting down my tears that can't help me. "I don't think there is." And I push my legs harder. Wishing I could run off the field and away.

If I thought things couldn't get worse, I was wrong. The day before our game, Mama and Daddy wake me up and tell me that Uncle Jack has been rushed back to the hospital. And that he's not likely to last long.

Of course they still make me go to school. "We'll come get you if need be," Daddy says.

All day between classes, I find myself rushing to the bathroom to cry. And I guess I look pretty rough: people stare at me in the halls, but nobody dares to ask what's wrong. Including Mr. Bonner. As I walk into language arts, he takes one glance at me and says, "I'm going to guess you're not in the mood to talk today?"

I just shake my head and take my seat.

As we continue to discuss *Monster,* my mind swirls. The main guy in the story, Steve, is accused of a bad crime, but he says he didn't do it. And even though the deck is stacked against him, he fights to maintain his innocence.

Something Great-Grampy JonJon *didn't* do. Because he didn't feel like he *could*.

It was all so unfair.

By the time the final bell of the school day rings, I've made up my mind. So once I'm in Mama's car and she signals to go left—toward the hospital—I speak up. "I have to go to practice."

"You don't today, sweetie," she says. "I've already spoken with Coach Natalie—"

"I *want* to go to practice. Our first state championship game is tomorrow morning, and I need to be there for my team. I'm the *captain,* Mama."

She takes a deep breath. "Love, I understand that. But this is more importan—"

"Not to me, it isn't," I say hard and fast.

You'd think I'd just confessed to being an alien her beloved daughter got swapped out with in her sleep. "Shenice, Uncle Jack is *dying*—"

"And I want to go to practice. I have to. It's my responsibility as a leader."

She doesn't respond.

"Remember what you told me when I was voted

captain and got scared? You said all I had to do was continue what I was already doing: keep my teammates' best interests at the top of my priority list. They need me, Mama. Even if I'm just cheering them on from the dugout."

"I understand that, baby, but this is family—"

"I don't even *know* him, Mama. I've met him, what, three times in my whole life? My *team* is more family to me than he is."

Now she looks like I slapped her.

"Please, just take me to practice."

She doesn't respond, but when the light turns green, she switches the blinker from left to right.

And even though I know this means I may never see Uncle Jack alive again, I exhale.

One step closer.

At the field, as soon as I'm out of the car, Mama speeds off just like I knew she would. And just as I hoped, the Firebus is parked where it usually is, so Mama didn't bother to check for grown-ups.

Because there aren't any here.

Practice doesn't start for another hour and a half, something I knew Mama wouldn't know because she and Daddy have been so preoccupied. The van is here because Coach Nat always leaves it parked at our field for the two nights before our final practice leading to a big game. It's one of her superstitions—I mean rituals.

I do walk onto the field so I can stash my schoolbooks and binders in the dugout, but once that's done, and I'm sure Mama has gotten far enough away, I take off in the direction of the house, my empty backpack pulled tight against my shoulders. I walk once I hit the main road, so as not to draw unnecessary attention, but when I reach T P Burruss Sr. Drive SW—aka Ashby Place—I break into a run again.

I don't stop until I get to the back of the house, and then I look around the yard for a decent-sized stick. Before leaving the other day, we pushed the plank against the gaping doorway but didn't secure it. Hoping no one renailed it into place during the three days I haven't been here.

I take a deep breath and reach forward.

It detaches with zero resistance.

Before I can think too much about what I'm doing, I've got the big stick in one hand and my phone in the other, and I'm trying to turn on the little flashlight. Which is when I realize my battery is only at 3 percent. I smack my forehead; there's totally a charging station with retractable cords in the dugout, but even going back to charge for five minutes would add fifteen to my mission. "Of *all* the times to forget to plug in, Lockwood." With the little light cranked up to 100 percent—because there's no way I'm going in there with it lower—my guess is I'll have all of ten minutes to look around.

I step inside. Slowly at first: no telling how strong these floors are. There's a good bit of creaking, but it seems fairly solid beneath the peeling plastic stuff in the kitchen. I think I heard Britt-Marie mutter something about being "appalled by the tacky linoleum they used to call flooring."

The living room has teal walls and hardwood floors, but I don't take the time to look around. I bank left into the little hallway and toward the two pitch-black bedrooms. The left one is wide open, but the door to the room on the right is almost closed.

I decide to start in there. My plan is to bang the end of the stick, which is about the length of Daddy's walking cane, against each floorboard to see if any of them sound hollow underneath. I don't even know if this is scientifically sound, but I feel like I saw it in a movie once.

I plunge into the darkness . . . and immediately scream and drop my phone as a group of bats whirl into a frenzy near the ceiling as soon as the light shines on them. I scrabble for the device, then back out of the room and pull the door *all* the way shut behind me, panting.

Please don't let that have been the right room.

Before entering the other space, I sweep the ceiling

to check for bats (*so* creepy). There are none, so I slowly step inside.

When I see the desk and dresser against the far wall, it occurs to me that the loose floorboard could be beneath a heavy piece of furniture I won't be able to move. Dread starts to creep in, but I do my best to shake it off so I can get started.

Phone is at 2 percent now.

First order of business in *this* room is easy: retrieve Valentina. She's on her side a couple yards in front of me, not too far from the room's right wall. I shrug off my backpack and rush forward, so I can carefully place her inside.

Which is when I see what made her tip over. In front of her, the corner of a warped floorboard is poking up.

My breath catches.

It takes some work and a few splinters, but I manage to get enough of a grip to lift the floorboard. . . .

There's a space beneath it, but nothing inside of it.

But then something pops into my head. A journal entry of Great-Grampy JonJon's: *Took a photograph with Jack in our childhood bedroom today. I think it's the only one we've ever taken together. Of course in the picture, he wanted to stand on his side of the room. . . .*

"Oh my god!" I say, hoping, hoping, *hoping* the picture he was referring to is the one in the trunk. In it, Jack is standing on the left . . . which would mean *his* side of the room would've been the left side.

I push the wonky floorboard back into place, then stand up to tap it with my stick. See what it sounds like.

Thunk, thunk.

Then the one beside it. (*Please let it sound different. . . .*)

Thack, thack.

Move to the left.

Thack, thack.

Thack, thack.

Thack, thack.

Few steps forward . . .

Thack, thack.

Thack, thack.

Back a bit, and a little farther to the left . . .

Thack, thack.

Thunk, thunk.

I freeze. (If I didn't know what it meant to have "my heart in my throat" before, I sure do now.) I tap again, harder this time.

THUNK, THUNK.

Before I can even register my own movements, I'm on my knees, phone light aimed at the ceiling, trying to get my fingernails under the loose floorboard.

The gap isn't wide enough for me to get a good grip.

I rush over to my backpack and take out the thin

metal ruler we use in geometry. And I return to my floorboard, shove it into the crack, and make a lever.

The floorboard pops up, and just like the other one, there's a space underneath.

Except this time it's not empty. There's something hidden there that looks as though it's wrapped in layers of that plastic wrap stuff my mom uses to cover leftover food in the fridge.

For a minute, I just kneel there staring at it. A little bit in shock.

Slowly, carefully, I reach for it. . . .

And then my light goes out.

18

Grand Slam

I make it through the first four innings of our state tournament game before my not-quite-completely-healed arm is throbbing so bad, I ask to be subbed out.

The only reason I was permitted to play at all is because there are camera crews here from every news network in the area. Turns out *everyone* is interested in "the heartwarming tale of a twelve-year-old softball player who risked life and limb to clear the name of her wrongfully disgraced great-grandfather, after discovering that his promising baseball career in the 1940s was ruined by a false accusation."

That's how the news anchor put it. There was an article in our city's biggest newspaper this morning, too.

I have to admit: groping through that dark house was the scariest thing I've ever done. For the first minute or so after my phone died, I just sat there, frozen in silence. I couldn't even breathe, I was so scared. The thing about being in darkness that *dark* is it seems like every sound has to be coming from some giant, many-fanged monster. And said monster is 100 percent right behind you, ready to devour you in a single bite if you move. Or breathe. Or blink.

But blink I did. And what I saw on the inside of my eyelids was Uncle Jack. First in that picture with Great-Grampy JonJon, and then in his hospital bed that last time he was there.

It didn't make the fear go away, but it did loosen my limbs. Took me about six seconds to feel my way into the space beneath the floorboard—and I *did* let out a tiny squeak when something crawled over my hand—but I managed to scoop up the plastic-wrapped package, feel for and grab my phone, crawl in the general direction of where I thought I left my backpack, slip the package in with Valentina, and creep toward the bedroom door. The moment I saw light, I *skedaddled*. (That word is from Drake, who uses it all the time when playing his video games.)

I even made it back to the field before anyone else got there. Which is where I left Valentina with a note to

Khyler and Hennessey, thanking them for what basically amounted to sacrificing her for *my* cause.

After plugging in my phone so I could get enough juice for it to power back on, I stuffed my schoolbooks back into my bag. And then I called Mama.

Who was crying when she answered.

Scared me half to the afterlife, but then she told me she was crying because of what I said. She hadn't even gone to the hospital yet. She was parked at the new strip mall up the road "nursing a macchiato" from the fancy coffee shop and "trying to process" my reasoning to see if I'd been "justified."

She came back to get me, and on the way to the hospital, I came clean. About everything.

Just made her cry even harder.

My hands shook the whole way up the elevator to Uncle Jack's floor. And I hugged the package, which I'd cleaned off with a bottle of water and a handful of napkins from Mama's glove compartment, tight to my chest as we moved through the hallways.

Then I did something I don't typically do: I prayed. That Uncle Jack would still be alive. (I assumed he was because Daddy hadn't called to say otherwise, but you never know.) That he'd be *awake* and *lucid*. And that when I held up the package, he would recognize it.

When Mama and I got into the room, Uncle Jack was asleep, and so was Daddy. My heart sank.

But then Mama woke Daddy up to let him know we'd arrived, and Daddy proceeded to wake Uncle Jack. And Mama didn't stop him.

Problem was, Uncle Jack didn't recognize anybody. His eyes were glazed over, and it was clear that he wasn't really *with* us.

But I went for it anyway.

"Uncle Jack? It's me, Shenice."

He slowly turned his head toward me.

"I brought you something." And I held up the package.

He looked at it, and a smile crept onto his face . . . but when he looked back at me, I could tell he didn't recognize it any more than he recognized us. "Well, isn't that nice?" he said. "Mighty kind of ya!"

"This is yours!" I said, injecting a little extra pep. "You hid it under the floorboard beneath where your bed used to be. In your childhood bedroom? Do you remember? I'm sure you do, right?"

"What is she talkin' about?" I heard Daddy ask Mama behind me. And Mama shushed him. Which I was thankful for . . . but then I felt a hand on my lower back.

"Shenice, baby," Mama said. "I understand that you're excited about what you found, but you gotta take it easy. Uncle Jack's not feeling great."

And something about that set me off. Because I *knew* Uncle Jack wasn't *feeling great*. He was *dying*. Like, right there in front of us. And there was nothing *easy* about any of it. Especially the part where I wound up with stitches in my catching arm trying to complete the mission Uncle Jack gave me, and then I still didn't give up *until I completed it.*

"This is what you told me I had to get, Uncle Jack!" I dropped down and immediately started pulling at the clouded plastic.

"Shenice . . . ," Mama called out behind me.

"One second, Mama. I have to get this open—"

"Shenice, honey . . ." Her hands landed on my shoulders, and I felt her crouch to my left. "We should go now, honey. This is a lot, and I think you've had enough."

I clawed at the hardened plastic so hard, I broke one of my chipped orange fingernails. "Oww!" And I put my finger in my mouth.

Which is when the tears started. Mama wrapped her arms around me, and I cracked as she pulled me to my feet. Big, heaving sobs about all of it: the death of Great-Grampy JonJon's ambitions, and the fact that Uncle Jack really *did* have proof of JonJon's innocence but couldn't use it. The incredible *unfairness* of it all.

I looked at Daddy, leaning on his cane, and thought about how the dream of playing professional baseball has just passed down, and down, and down . . . and gone unaccomplished.

How Uncle Jack won't ever get to see a Lockwood achieve what his big brother was after.

I took a deep breath and pulled myself together. My tears weren't going to bring Uncle Jack back to *our* reality, and they certainly weren't going to keep him from passing away. I had the package now, and there was no reason for me to doubt the glove was inside it when everything else Jack said had been true. I needed to *do* something with it.

And then it hit me.

"Hey, Daddy?" I said. "You still have that friend who works at the *Fulton Journal Constitution?*"

From there, things moved pretty quickly. We stopped at the nurse's station, and they let me use a pair of scissors to cut a slit in the plastic, but I didn't rip it off right there like I'd been trying to in the room. I don't think Uncle Jack would've recognized it at that point.

It wasn't until I got in Mama's car that I removed the wrapping and revealed the shoebox-sized, smooth wooden box with a hinged lid and tarnished metal clasp. I opened it slowly, and when I saw what was inside (in addition to a *very* old stuffed bunny rabbit, a Babe Ruth baseball card, and a bag of multicolored marbles), I did my best to keep my cool. Just took Mama's phone and called Daddy's friend at the newspaper—a former college baseball teammate just like the doctor who stitched me up had been. As soon as I gave him a rundown of the story—and told him I had the DiMaggio glove—he requested to speak to Mama and asked if he could meet us at the house.

After he and I talked, he took some pictures of me and the glove, then left. And not twenty minutes later, the phone rang: a reporter at one of the local TV stations had heard about our story and wanted to know more. And after she asked more about *me* and found out I'm the captain of the first all-Black 12U fast-pitch softball team to make it to the state tournament, the calls didn't stop for hours.

So here we are.

I gave the game my all for as long as I could, since, you know, I was gonna be on TV. But once I hit my limit, I was done. (Thankfully they're including the part about the stitches in the story.)

Top of the sixth, and we're down two runs. Not impossible to come back from. Bases are loaded, but there are two outs, and Cala just threw a strike. Two more of those, and we'll change sides and have a shot at a comeback.

Still, though, I find that I care a bit less than a *softball captain on the news* probably should. Too many other things on my mind.

Like Uncle Jack. Who is still hanging on—no more *lucid* than he was when I tried to show him his box, but still alive. And where it seemed like before, no one knew anything about the *illustrious* (thanks, Mr. Bonner) Jumpin' JonJon Lee Lockwood, Negro Southern League legend and *almost* MLB player, they can certainly learn about him now: his story is officially on the internet.

A *CLINK* snatches me back to our game. The Henry County Hurricane stands erupt with cheers: their batter just smashed the ball out into deep left field.

I shoot to my feet. Cortlin is running as hard as she can, but she's not gonna catch it.

"Dang it!" Ms. Erica whisper-shouts beside me.

The batter's foot lands on third a split second before the ball hits Hennessey's glove.

"SAFE!" The ump says.

A beautiful triple with three RBIs. Hurricanes are officially up by five.

I don't think we're gonna win this game.

The next batter hits a pop fly, and Khyler snatches it out of the air.

"Change sides!" the ump shouts (as if we don't know that already). And soon Hennessey and Khyler are sitting down on my left, as Britt-Marie and Laury flank my right.

"We're definitely not gonna win this game," Laury says.

"A little louder for the people in the back," from Britt-Marie. "Sucks."

It's quiet for a few seconds, and then: "I'm mad . . . but also not sure I'm *as* mad as I feel like I maybe *should* be?" says Khyler. "I *want* to win. Really bad. But I also don't know that we can? We *were* trash in practice last week. . . ."

"It's all my fault," I say. "I was distracted, and I distracted y'all—"

"Hey now, I'm almost a teenager," Laury says. "*I* decide what I *allow* to distract me. Thank you very much."

"I would've done the same thing you did, Lightning," Hennessey chimes in. "When you know somebody is dying, and they ask you for something . . . you do it." Her eyes drop, and Khyler wraps an arm around Hen's shoulders. "I *did* want to win, even just to make my dad proud. But what you were doing felt super important. And I think he would've been proud of me helping with that, too. As much as I hate losing—"

"And you *certainly* hated losing Valentina," Khyler cuts in.

There's a brief moment of silence, and then all of us burst out laughing.

"We *did* win section, ladies. There's always next year for State," Britt-Marie says.

"True. And this season was certainly an adventure," Laury says.

Britt-Marie takes off her helmet and shakes out her curls. "And now we get to be on TV."

"All thanks to our mighty captain." Khyler nudges me in the side.

"We're glad you found what you were looking for, Shan-Shan," says Laury.

"Yeah," from Hennessey. "Even though you almost double murdered yourself *and* our beloved Valentina. Hmph."

We all laugh again. It's almost Khyler's turn at bat. And even though I know it's probably the cheesiest thing I'll ever say, before she gets up, I tell them: "I'm just glad to have friends like y'all."

We do *not* win the game.

And Quickfire Cala is the most furious about it.

Even her anger doesn't last long, though. As soon as we finish congratulating the Hurricanes, we collapse into a huddle, all crying like big babies.

"We had a good run this season, didn't we?" Noelle says, dabbing at her eyes.

"Heck yes, we did," from Laury. "First all-Black team to take DYSA district *and* section titles? We're the grooviest gals around!"

"Wow, Laury. That's next-level ridiculous, even from you," Hennessey says.

We all laugh.

"Mellow Mushroom?" says Britt-Marie. She sucks in a huge sniffle that sounds super nasty.

Coach Nat loosens the circle, then looks around at

each of us in turn. "Absolutely," she says. "You can each eat as many slices as you want. You'll need the fuel for practice tomorrow." She leans in. "It's gonna be a real doozy, friends."

"Awww, Coach! Come on!" Hennessey says. "Give us a break!"

"Oh, I am!" Coach Nat says, patting me and Britt-Marie on our backs. "We're gonna *break* out of this tendency to let distractions get the best of us. Head in the flames, right?" And she winks one of those strange blue eyes. "I'll see you all at the van."

She struts away.

"Brutal," Cortlin says.

"You can say that again," from Clementine.

I smile. "Well, it looks like we'll have no choice *but* to rise from the ashes, Firebirds."

"Wow, our captain is corny," Britt-Marie say.

"Whatever. You love it," I reply. "To the Firebus!"

April 25, 2021

Dear Great-Grampy JonJon,

I hope this isn't blasphemy (I learned that word in my language arts class. Are you impressed with me yet?), me writing in your journal. Yes, I also read it, but that's beside the point. What matters is that I am your great-granddaughter, Shenice "Lightning" Lockwood, and I just spent the past few weeks working to clear your name.

It's too long a story for me to write in here, especially since there's a chance you and your little brother, Jack, are together again in whatever nice place we go after we're not in our Earth bodies anymore, and he's already told you everything. But suffice it to say—that's a phrase my best friend Britt-Marie uses a lot—that the sour green-with-too-much-envy white dude who tried to ruin your legacy did NOT succeed.

In fact, the opposite happened. I'm sure this is going to sound nuts since you lived your whole life without the internet (no idea HOW, by the way—if the Wi-Fi goes out for fifteen minutes, I basically can't function), but after losing in the first round of the state softball tournament yesterday, on the way to the van, my team was approached by a short white lady.

Turns out, she's the granddaughter of Jacob Carlyle. Kathleen is her name.

Can you even <u>believe</u> that??

It gets better, too: she saw an article about me online—your great-granddaughter is a local celebrity now—and my story matched one her dad told her about her grandpa when she was young, and she'd lost all her friends after deciding to play with the one Black girl in her second-grade class. "It was 1965," she said. "There were a lot of people here in Georgia who couldn't seem to get okay with the integration of schools, but that story about Grandpa Jake and the awful thing he did to your great-grandfather made me lean in a little harder."

She also said she never met her grandpa. He and his son (her dad) stopped speaking due to "differences of opinion about Black people." He died before she got the chance to see if he'd had a change of heart. "But I knew I never wanted to be <u>anything</u> like a man who would do what my father said Grandpa Jake did."

When she saw that we Firebirds would be playing in the state tournament, she decided to come to the game.

Then she said something that stunned us all: "If you all are willing to receive it, I'd like to give you some of the money he left behind. You probably don't even need it, but I'd really love to do something that would make him roll over in his grave, you know?" And she winked.

None of us said anything.

"I hope that wasn't insulting!" she continued, wringing her hands. "I just thought maybe you could use it on whatever you want. Additional uniforms? Maybe some unnecessary and overpriced equipment?"

"Yo . . . we could all get that Louisville Slugger joint homegirl from the Stockwood Sharks had," my teammate Laury said. "The one Britt got."

It made Kathleen smile. "That's the spirit!" she said. "So whattaya say? Wanna blow a chunk of a dead monster's cash? Disturb his rotten soul a little bit?"

"Oh, I think I like her," my best friend, Britt-Marie, said with a grin.

"How much we talking?" (That was our pitcher, Cala.)

"Cala! Rude!" Hennessey (third base) said.

"What? I wanna know!"

Kathleen laughed again. "Man, you loves got SPUNK." And she did a little shimmy.

Her answer: Seventy-five. THOUSAND. Dollars.

"That's a good chunk for each of you," she said. "And you can do whatever the heck you want with it, provided you get parent or guardian approval. Live your best lives, babies!"

"Oh yeah, I DEFINITELY like her," Khyler (shortstop) chimed in.

By the time we finished our post-game pizza, word had gotten around to all the parents, and it was decided that Coach Nat would receive the donation and distribute it to each of us as Firebird scholarships.

Which . . . is sorta wack because I'd really prefer to get a new bike, phone, and laptop.

But fine. Consolation prize: they all also agreed that we'd each get $100 in spending money. Oh, and Ms. Kathleen is buying the whole team that bat on top.

So there you have it! OH! ALSO! Most important part: guess who is being inducted into the Negro Leagues Baseball Museum after all?

That's right: YOU.

They're even making a temporary exhibit about you, where some of the stuff from the attic and your trunk will be on display. People can push a button to hear a recording of your story. (Nobody does those plaque thingies at museums anymore.)

And they're including the DiMaggio glove, which I am letting them BORROW. Because as it turns out, since the glove was donated and never sold, the last person to possess it is considered its rightful owner. And that person left it to ME in his will. I'm thinking about selling it on this auction website called eBid. (I'm telling you, Great-Grampy, the internet is amazing.) Haven't decided yet.

Anyway, just wanted you to know all that. I'll stop "desecrating" this sacred book and put it back in your trunk now.

Last but not least, I want to say thank you. Not to get all sappy, but I'm pretty sure my passion for "batball," as my little brother calls it (which you maybe already know), wouldn't exist without you passing it down in our Lockwood blood. I can say for CERTAIN that I definitely (literally) wouldn't exist without you.

And though I can't guarantee that the ball-playing gene will continue in my children—if I wind up having any—I can promise that your TRUE legacy will live on forever now.

Or at least as long as there is such a thing as the internet.

Rest in peace, Great-Grampy JonJon. For real this time.

And tell Uncle Jack I said same to him if you happen to see him around.

Sincerely,

Your Favorite Great-Granddaughter,

Shenice 'Lightning' Lockwood
⚡

ACKNOWLEDGMENTS

(Why are these things always so much harder to write than the actual book?! **huffs**)

Okay. If you're reading this and you *know* you contributed to this book in some way but I don't mention you, please don't be too mad at me. I am writing these acknowledgments while trying to finish another book, plan a third, and script a podcast. So cut ya girl some slack.

Great!

I will start with the guy who always creates the space for me to create: Nigel Livingstone. I appreciate you and your willingness to not only let me chase my dreams, but to hold down the fort and egg me on as I do. Couldn't do any of this without you.

To my littles, Kiran and Milo: Thank you for going to bug Daddy when Mommy tells you she's working and you have to get out of her office.

My beloved editor, Phoebe Yeh: I am getting better at this, and it's largely because you're such a hardass and won't let me slack off or phone anything in. I guess that's what happens when you're edited by the woman who has a Magic School Bus character literally named for her.

Agent Rena Rossner: Thank you for selling this thing.

Agent Mollie Glick: Thank YOU for always holding me down (in the very positive hip-hoppish way).

Brittany Marie Hogan, Monica Douglass, Michael Bonner, Natalie Pendley, and Erica Bundy: Thank you for letting me literally put you in my book. Like . . . as yourselves. You have been immortalized! Also to Natalie: thank you for combing through this thing to check my softball stuff since it's been literally eighteen years since I've played (aging is traaaaash).

Laury and Hennessey (surnames redacted because they are minors as of the writing of these acknowledgments): I appreciate you allowing me to borrow your names for characters.

Breanna McDaniel: Whew, CHILD, this book would be awful without your input! Thank you thank you thank you for putting your critical eye on it and pointing out the weak spots and just being an amazing critique pal and friend. I love yooooou!

And my RHCB crew: KD, Aunt Barb, Queen Judith, Lizzy, Dom, Schiz, Nemesis-Bestie Adamo, Kells, Jules, Caitlin, Adrienne, Carol, Ward, Kam, and Kolani. I love you all in a home run way.

(Yes, that was corny. Deal with it.)

ABOUT THE AUTHOR

NIC STONE is the *New York Times* bestselling author of *Clean Getaway,* which received starred reviews from *Publishers Weekly* and *Booklist,* who called it "an absolute firecracker of a book." She is also the author of the number one *New York Times* bestselling and William C. Morris Award finalist *Dear Martin,* its *New York Times* best-selling sequel *Dear Justyce,* and the acclaimed novels *Odd One Out* and *Jackpot* for teens.

Nic spent several years on the softball field as a kid, and *Fast Pitch* grew out of her love of the sport and the movie *The Sandlot,* and her desire to see more Black female athletes represented on the field and on the page.

Nic lives in Atlanta with her adorable little family.

nicstone.info
: @nicstone